HORNS & H

By

Jayne Gooding

BMP
Blue Mendos Publications

Published by Blue Mendos Publications
In association with Amazon KdP Publishing

Published in paperback 2022
Category: Fiction
Copyright Jayne Gooding © 2022
ISBN : 9798849848556

Cover design by Jill Rinaldi © 2022

All rights reserved, Copyright under Berne Copyright Convention and Pan American Convention. No part of this book may be reproduced, stored in a retrieval system, or transmitted in any form or by any means, electronic, mechanical, photocopying, recording or otherwise, without prior permission of the author. The author's moral rights have been asserted.

This is a work of fiction. Names, characters, corporations, institutions, organisations, events or locales in this novel are either the product of the author's imagination or, if real, used fictitiously. Any resemblance to actual persons (living or dead) is entirely coincidental.

Dedication

For Karen and remembering the happy times.

Acknowledgement

Jill Rinaldi for designing the book cover.

Chapter 1

The taxi came to a halt outside the Laughing Heart wine bar on the Hackney Road in East London. Star Bellamy reached into her handbag for her vanity mirror, her heart thumping with nervous anticipation. There was a ritual of mixed emotions she had to work through on first dates.

"I hope I like her. Maybe she is the one," thought Star. *"I hope she likes me! What if she doesn't? What if she doesn't like police officers? Come on, Star, pull yourself together!"*

Star had opted to meet Julia at the Laughing Heart wine bar because it wasn't action orientated. They would be able to find a quiet place to just sit and chat and if it became apparent quite early on that there was no spark, Star had the option to make her excuses and leave. If, however, they were getting along famously, she had the option to stay longer and let the evening unfold as it should. Star had learnt that there were no hard and fast rules to dating, no template to follow to find that one special, elusive, person to share a life with.

"If it doesn't go as I hope, at least I'll have made another friend," she mused as she checked her lip gloss.

"I hope I haven't over done it with this dress," Star thought as she handed a twenty-pound note to the black cab driver.

"Keep the change," she said with a smile.

"Cheers darling," said the Cabbie. "I hope you don't mind me saying but you look a million dollars. Whoever he is, he's a lucky guy."

"Thank you," Star said with a chuckle.

"I can just imagine his face if I'd told him that I'm meeting a girl," she thought.

Star got out of the black cab and closed the door firmly. She caught a reflection of herself in an adjacent shop's window. The new cobalt blue, structured stretch ruffle, knee-length dress she had bought from Karen Millen hung perfectly on her supple, curvaceous, figure. She placed her hands on her hips while looking herself up and down. Her long russet brown hair toppled over her shoulders and framed her heart shaped face. She took a deep breath, opened the door and entered the wine bar; the pivotal moment had arrived.

"Good evening, Madam," the waiter said, as he passed by carrying an ice bucket.

"Good evening," Star replied with a smile.

Star was drawn to a beautiful woman with lavish sun-gold hair that cascaded over her shoulders. The blonde raised her hand and waved. It was Julia, her date for the evening. Star beamed and waved back. As she approached the table, she couldn't help but notice her unblemished skin with a peaches and cream complexion.

"Wow, Julia is even more attractive than her online profile," thought Star.

"You must be Star," said Julia. "You look amazing!"

"Thank you, so do you," Star said as she admired her black Geo Jacquard Belted Peplum Mini Dress.

"Karen Millen?" said Julia.

Star nodded.

"It looks like we both have good taste," Star said.

The two women shook hands. Star sat with her back to the bare brick wall.

"This was an excellent choice, Star. I've passed it many times and often promised myself a visit," Julia said as she raised her glass.

"You probably noticed that the wine list started with a Keats poem. It was that and the fact that the wines are all sourced from lesser-known vineyards which attracted me to the place," Star said.

"The wine is excellent," Julia said, "Is it organic?"

"It is," Star said with a warm smile.

"Good evening. My name is Claude and I'll be your waiter this evening. Have you had an opportunity to view our wine list?"

"Can you choose for us Star?" Julia asked, as she handed Star the wine list.

"Do you prefer red, white, rosé or fizz?"

"Definitely red please," Julia said.

Star handed the waiter the wine list.

"Can we have a bottle of the 2016 Vinteloper Odeon Pinot Noir, Claude, thank you," said Star.

"That is an excellent choice madam."

"It's an Australian wine from the Adelaide Hills," Star said. "I hope you like it."

"I'm sure I will," Julia replied.

Claude returned with the bottle of Vinteloper. He uncorked the bottle and poured a small measure for Star to taste.

"Hmm, that's lovely," Star said.

Claude filled both glasses.

"If I can be of any further assistance, please do not hesitate to call me over," Claude said as he placed the bottle onto the table.

"Thank you, Claude," Star replied.

Julia raised her glass.

"It's wonderful to finally meet you, Star, and you are every bit as lovely as your profile picture.

"Cheers," Julia said.

"Cheers," Star said.

"Have you been on the dating site long?" Julia said, peering over the top of her wine glass.

"I've met a few people through the site and made some new friends," Star said. "What is it that you do?"

"I'm a primary school teacher during the day, but at night I sing with a band," Julia said.

"Wow, that is so interesting," Star said.

"Which part, being a schoolteacher or singing with a band?" Julia said with a cheeky grin.

"Both. Well, playing in a band of course," Star said with a giggle.

"I like Julia. She's fun and a little mischievous," thought Star.

"We're an all-girl group and call ourselves the Pride Mantras. We've only played a couple of paying gigs but it's not about the money," Julia said as she shook her head. "I would love to say that it's about making a political point that benefits the LGBT community, but to be honest, Star, I just like to sing."

"I'd like to come and listen to you guys. When are you playing again?"

"I said I like to sing but that doesn't necessarily mean that I'm any good at it," chuckled Julia. "We don't have any firm dates, but you'd be very welcome. Okay, enough about me what about you?"

"Okay, right. I'm thirty-one years of age. My mother was Portuguese, and my father was British."

"That explains your beautiful olive skin and vivacious chestnut brown eyes. I'm sorry, Star, I interrupted you. Please continue," Julia said as she drank the last of her wine.

"I've lived in London most of my life and I'm a police officer," Star said, then paused waiting for Julia's response.

"Oh my! A beautiful, gay, police officer. I'm beginning to think all my prayers may have been answered. Quick, pinch me! I may be dreaming," Julia said as she refilled her glass.

"Thank you, but I'm not gay. I'm bi-sexual. Is that a problem for you?" Star said as she put her glass on the table.

"No, not at all. I'm just intrigued, how did you know you were bi?"

"I didn't have the slightest inkling for many years. I was lucky to have had a wide circle of friends that included both girls and boys," Star said as she topped up her glass. "I never thought about girls as anything other than being my friends. However, I did, like almost every girl in my class, have a crush on Michael Woods. The girls would obsess over Michael during break times and talk about holding his hand or stealing a kiss down by the coat lockers. Michael, on the other hand, had no time for any of us girls and would play football with his friends every break time. I do remember going to the cinema with friends to watch a movie called 'Match Point'. It was about a former tennis pro who falls for an actress who happened to be dating his friend. I found myself sexually attracted to Scarlett Johannsson. She plagued my thoughts for days after seeing the movie, but in the end, I concluded that maybe it was because I wanted to be as sexy and attractive as she is. Then, just like that, it was forgotten until I was seventeen. Like most girls, I began to have fantasies and desires but almost half of them were about girls. It began to worry me and almost subconsciously I forced myself into a state of denial. I didn't dare share my thoughts with friends, but instead convinced myself that it was something everyone went through because it was sexually exciting and different. I was living a lie and it wasn't until I was twenty-two and seeing this guy that I just couldn't ignore it anymore. It was like an epiphany. I could finally acknowledge that I wasn't happy in my relationships and could no longer deny my sexuality. It was time to open my eyes and accept that I simply wasn't the same as everyone else."

"Good for you, Star!" Julia said.

"It wasn't easy, Julia as I'm sure you'd appreciate, because I was neither gay nor straight. So in effect, I had given myself two things to think about. The first being that I was bi-sexual and the second being that I might just be confused, undecided or simply curious? In the early days I had taken a step back from my circle of friends and when I wasn't working, I'd torment myself with negative thoughts. I worried that being bi-sexual meant that I could never be happy with either a man or a woman. I thought about children and whether or not I wanted them. In short, Julia, I gave myself a list as long as your arm of things I could worry about. I felt alone and vulnerable as I'd been bottling all my emotions up," Star said.

"I'm so sorry to hear that, Star," Julia said kindly.

"It was a difficult time. I was becoming increasingly anxious and depressed. It was then that I decided to take control of my thoughts. The only way I could do this was to talk about it. At first the conversation was with strangers so I could gauge their reaction, and then finally I spoke with another police officer who I had been at Hendon Training College with. We were having a drink one night in a bar after our shift ended and I just blurted it out. She was truly wonderful and understanding and then confided that she was gay and hadn't told anyone for fear of being laughed at, gossiped about or victimised by some senior police officer with out-dated Neanderthal views from the dark ages. My friend Jayne was a tremendous support and she helped me realise you can only be truly happy and fulfilled when you acknowledge who you are," Star said.

"She sounds fabulous. What happened to her?"

"We still keep in touch, but Jayne transferred to Brighton about five or six years ago. She's happy, in a loving, caring, relationship and has made Sergeant. I'm pleased for her," Star said.

"Were you two together?"

"Not in the sense that we were together as an item," Star said.

"I'm sorry, I didn't mean to offend you," Julia said.

"I'm not offended Julia," Star said as she shook her head and smiled. "I came to realise that the right people will accept me for who I am."

"Damn right!" Julia said.

"What about you, Julia?"

"What, being gay?"

Star nodded.

"I knew from a very early age that I was different. I had no interest in playing with dolls, kiss chase, or flirting with boys. I would spend my summer holidays working with horses down at the stables. In return for feeding and mucking out I got to ride the horses for free. There was a girl, a very pretty girl with these luminous jade green eyes and rouge red hair that spiralled down over her shoulders. She was a couple of years older than me, and I found myself watching her every move, admiring her every curve, and then one day she caught me."

"What did she say?" Star said, placing her hand over her glass as Julia reached over and tried to top it up.

"Nothing, she just smiled, and my knees went weak, my mouth was dry, and I could hear every beat of my heart thumping loud and clear. After we finished all our duties we both just lay out on the hay and chatted. Finally, as the sun went down, she sat bolt upright, leant over and kissed me. That was my first sexual experience with a girl, and I embraced my sexuality head on by reaching out to the LGBT community and engaging with others like me."

"Well done, you!" Star said.

"This girl is amazing. I hope I didn't mess it up by going on about being bi," thought Star.

"Thank you, Star. Tell me, what do you do in the police force? I think every little girl at some point has dreamed about becoming a police officer," Julia said.

Star stood up.

"Can you excuse me for five minutes? I need to visit the ladies' room," Star said.

Julia smiled. "Of course, shall I order another bottle of wine?"

Star nodded and headed across the wine bar to the ladies' room.

The ladies' room was empty. Star put her handbag on the marble worktop and checked her reflection in the mirror.

"What do I do? Do I suggest we go back to my place for a coffee or slow things down and aim for a second date?" thought Star.

As she applied her lipstick, she felt a familiar buzzing sensation in her ears. She clasped her chest as it began to tighten. The ladies' room had grown cold. Star felt a presence behind her. She turned abruptly and caught a glimpse of a figure in her peripheral vision. The temperature had plummeted. The toilet door slammed shut and the lights dimmed. Star turned back to the mirror and put her lipstick back into her handbag. The lights began to flicker. As she turned to leave, the translucent apparition of an elderly woman stood before her.

"Please help my son, he is in danger!"

The apparition disappeared, the temperature returned to normal, and the lights stopped flickering.

Star Bellamy was an extremely powerful psychic like her mother before her. She had been born with extrasensory perception. Her gifts had grown year after year, with the first spirit calling on her for help when she was just twelve years old. It had been the desire to help the lost and needy souls that had first prompted her to join the police force.

Star took a deep breath and composed herself. She picked up her handbag and returned to the wine bar.

"You were going to tell me about the police force," Julia said.

Star looked at her wine glass. Julia had refilled it.

"I'm a Detective Sergeant with the Criminal Investigation Department. That's CID for short," Star said as she reached for her glass.

"I wonder who that was trying to contact me," thought Star.

"A Detective! I'm impressed. You must see a lot in your job," Julia said.

"We only investigate serious crimes." Star said.

"Like what?"

"Murder, serious assault, robberies and sexual offences," Star said.

"Oh my, you're the real deal. Hold on, do you have someone above you?"

Star nodded slowly.

"I knew it. Don't tell me it's a man."

Star nodded again.

"I bet he's bloody useless at his job and takes the credit for what you do," Julia said.

"I couldn't say," Star said coyly.

"You don't have to, Star. I can see it now. Some fifty-year-old white male that's part of the old boy network."

"You know him then," Star said as she chuckled.

"Watch what you're saying here, Star. Detective Inspector Ronald Pratt may be a relic from a bygone age with his cheap, food-stained suits and greasy hair but he's still your boss and guvnor and don't forget that," thought Star.

"Have you ever worked on crimes that have been on television or in the newspapers?" Julia asked as she put her elbows on the table and rested her head in her hands.

Star found herself staring at Julia's siren red fingernails and dimpled chin.

"Probably, but I'm not really at liberty to discuss them," Star said.

Julia sat upright.

"Sorry, I didn't mean to intrude," Julia said bluntly.

"No, *I'm* sorry, Julia. Whenever there are on-going prosecutions, I'm just not allowed to discuss them. I wasn't being awkward."

Julia smiled warmly and relaxed her posture.

"How do you feel tonight's date has gone?" Julia asked, as she smiled and tilted her head.

"I've had a wonderful evening and enjoyed meeting you," Star said.

"But?"

Star shook her head and grinned.

"There are no buts. I was going to ask you if we could go out again, only next time to a restaurant," Star said.

"Okay, well I definitely feel a connection between us, and I'm pleased we're not going down the 'how many days should I hold off before calling her without sounding desperate' route."

"I wouldn't do that, and I feel there's something between us too. I believe in being honest in matters of the heart. If there was no special spark there, then I would ask if we could remain friends. I would never, ever say that I would call someone and then not see it through. That's just plain cruel," Star said. "I like you Julia, and I don't want to rush anything. I sense that we are both looking for more than an adventurous liaison."

"Hey, I like you too."

Star motioned for Claude, the waiter, to bring the bill. Julia reached into her handbag and pulled out her purse.

Star held out her hand to stop her. "I would like to get this Julia. I've had a wonderful evening and I'm looking forward to seeing you again soon," she said.

"Thank you, Star, but I insist on paying next time," Julia said.

"Oh good, I'll book the Dorchester then," Star said, chuckling.

"Sounds fabulous, will you book one room or two?" Julia replied softly.

"You are naughty Miss Julia Portman," Star said as she handed her credit card to the waiter.

"I certainly can be," Julia said and winked slowly.

Star handed Claude a tip as he returned the credit card.

The two women stood outside the wine bar in the cold night air. It was just after 10.00pm. Star raised her hand and a black cab pulled over. Out of the corner of her eye, she spotted the apparition of the old woman from the ladies' toilets. She was pointing at a man wearing a suit and carrying a suitcase.

"When will you call?" Julia said as she gracefully entered the taxi.

"Definitely the day after tomorrow, Julia," Star said as Julia got into the taxi and closed the door.

As the cab moved away Star looked back across the road. Several steps behind the businessman was a young man in his mid-twenties. He wore dark coloured jeans and a black hoodie. A deep sense of dread began to manifest itself. The apparition pointed at the young man. She began to cross the road. A car tooted its horn and the driver mouthed obscenities. Star watched as the young man lifted the hood over his head. She could see him reaching into his trouser top and pull out a long knife. There was a high-pitched buzzing emanating from the apparition.

"Hey, you!" Star called out.

The young man in the hoodie didn't hear her. He raised the knife and ran forward, plunging the knife into the back of the businessman. The piercing scream from the apparition was overwhelming. Star slipped off her high heels, hitched up her skirt and began to race up the pavement towards the attacker. Over and over the young man thrust the blade into his victim. The businessman dropped his case and slumped to the ground.

"Stop, police!" Star yelled out.

The attacker turned back to see Star racing towards him. He dropped the knife and bolted across the road. A white van came screeching to a halt, narrowly missing him. Star was hot on his heels. The attacker bumped into a young woman. She bounced against the wall, tripped and fell to the ground. Star raced past her. The attacker turned sharply to his right and down into an alleyway. There was just the one street light. The end of the alleyway had been sealed off with a three-metre brick wall. The attacker ran towards the wall. He leapt into the air and reached out for the top of the wall. As he clung to the wall, trying desperately to clamber up to the top, Star reached up and took a firm grip of his ankle. She tugged with all the strength she could muster. The attacker lost his grasp and slid down the wall. He quickly clambered to his feet.

"I am Detective Sergeant Star Bellamy, and you are under arrest," Star panted, as she tried to catch her breath and compose herself.

"Fuck you Five-O!" yelled the attacker as he clenched his fists.

Star closed her eyes momentarily before drawing on her extensive martial art training. She assumed the Muay Thai square stance. Unlike karate where the side stance is predominately designed for moving back and forth to block or miss an attacker's strike, the square stance is for attacking and standing your ground.

"Get out of my way or die, Five-O!" the attacker snarled.

Star stood firm and faced the attacker. He lunged forward with a clumsy punch. Star let loose with a deadly combination. She quickly raised her knee while turning her supporting foot and the rest of her body in a semi-circular motion, extending her leg and striking the side of the attacker's mid-section. The attacker was knocked off balance. Star followed up with a precise and forceful jab to his chin. The attacker's legs crumpled beneath him as he fell unconscious to the concrete.

Star did her basic police self-defence training but soon discovered in her first altercation with a known villain that it was ineffective against a criminal fighting for his freedom. Her colleague recommended Jiu Jitsu, as most of her brawls ended up in rolling around on the floor. However, Star was drawn to Muay Thai because it focused on striking with fists, legs, knees and elbows. She was advised against it to avoid complaints for using excessive force but continued with her training anyway. In 21st century London, where heavily armed and dangerous gangs with no respect for the law are responsible for savage armed robberies, brutal murders, drug offences and burglaries, Star concluded that she needed to be able to protect herself effectively.

"Are you okay?"

It was a waiter from a nearby restaurant.

"I saw you giving chase and thought you might need help," he said.

"It's all under control, thank you," Star said as she turned the attacker over and forced his arms up behind his back. "I'm a police officer. Can you please call 999 for back up and an ambulance?"

Chapter 2

Ty Patterson was handcuffed and transported to the nearest police station in Hackney. He was taken into the custody suite where he was searched. He was found to have a wallet that included a driver's licence, four hundred and sixty pounds, and a photograph of a woman. They were removed and stored in a secure locker. A more intimate search had been ordered as the officers had reason to believe that Ty was in possession of drugs. None were found.

Star Bellamy, being the arresting officer and also witness to the murder of Mr Alan Chambers, accountant, age 42 from Stratford, London E15, provided the custody sergeant with sufficient evidence to charge Ty Patterson.

"Mr Ty Patterson, I am the custody sergeant. It is my job to inform you of your rights."

"Fuck you!" he said.

"Is there anyone you would like me to inform of your arrest?"

"No!"

"Sir, you are entitled to free legal advice. Would you like me to organise that for you?"

"I'm not guilty. Your officer has made a dreadful mistake," Ty snarled.

"Would you like to view the police code of practice?"

"A life changing, dreadful mistake," he snarled again.

"This written notice confirms the rights I have already outlined. In addition, it confirms your right to adequate food and drink, access to a toilet, reasonable standards of physical comfort and medical attention if you're feeling ill," the custody sergeant said as he placed a custody record in front of Ty. "Can you sign here please?"

"Fuck you, Five-O."

The custody sergeant noted his refusal to sign on the custody sheet.

Ty was taken to have his fingerprints, photographs and a DNA sample done.

"Sir, I'd like your consent to carry out these procedures," the officer said.

"I ain't giving you shit!" Ty yelled through gritted teeth.

"I'll ask you again, sir, and I must inform you that it is our right to use reasonable force should you not grant your consent," the officer said.

"Out there on the streets I'd tear you and all you Feds to shreds," Ty snarled.

The officer looked over Ty's shoulder at two uniformed police officers and beckoned them over. They took a firm grip of his arm and hand until the fingerprints were taken. Ty continued to be confrontational until the process was complete and was then taken to a cell.

Meanwhile back in Hackney, Star had called in a team to secure the area for evidence. The knife was bagged, and CCTV footage obtained, clearly showing the unprovoked attack on the victim, Mr Alan Chambers. Once she arrived back at the station, she was surprised to find Detective Inspector Pratt was already there.

"Bellamy, where are we with this?" DI Pratt said.

Star brought her superior officer up to speed.

"Good, that's another dent in knife crime statistics," DI Pratt said, placing both hands on his hips. "Let's get this wrapped up."

"Sir, I think there's more to this," Star said.

"What do you mean more? We have an eyewitness and CCTV to collaborate your statement. That's it," DI Pratt said, shaking his head impatiently.

Star placed a file on the desk

"Those upstairs want us to make inroads into the knife crime that's been plaguing our city. We had over three thousand knife related arrests last year and over one hundred and fifty murdered. The uniforms are making ten arrests a day and still we're just scratching the surface. Get this Ty Patterson wrapped up and let's move on to the next case," DI Pratt said.

'You are a bloody dinosaur. And what's with the soup-stained suit?" thought Star.

"Sir, I've been looking at Ty Patterson's record and something just doesn't add up," Star said, as she put the sheets out on the desk. "Ty Patterson is from Croydon, an area notorious for the postcode gang wars. He was arrested and found guilty of the murder of a rival gang member twelve months ago. Four masked men invaded his home and stabbed him thirty-six times. Ty and three others were arrested. Two of the four were sentenced to twenty years for murder and a third was sentenced to ten years for manslaughter. Ty Patterson walked away having been found not guilty. Sir, he has a rap sheet as long as your arm dating back to his school days, and all have been in and around the Croydon area. I believe the question is why was Ty Patterson in Hackney and why did he murder an accountant on his way home from work," Star said.

"Fine, ask your questions but don't give him an inch. I know the sort, he'll take a mile and slip through the net again," DI Pratt said firmly. "Keep me posted."

"Yes sir," Star said.

Star checked her watch. It was just after midnight. She went down to the interview room where Ty had been kept waiting. She opened the door. He sat at the table with his head down. She pulled out the wooden chair and sat opposite him. She placed her file on the desk and turned on the recording equipment. She stated her name as the interviewing officer, the time, date and location of the interview.

"Mr Ty Patterson, this interview will be recorded. You do not have to say anything. But it may harm your defence if you do not mention, when questioned, something which you later rely on in court. Anything you do say may be given in evidence."

"Ty, where were you this evening at 10.10pm?" Star asked.

"No comment," said Ty.

"Would I be correct in saying that you were on the Lauriston Road in Hackney?"

"Not me, must have been someone else. I mean we all look the same to you lot, don't we?"

"If it wasn't you Mr Ty Patterson, can you please tell me where you were?"

"No comment to that question or any other questions you may have," Ty said calmly.

Star reached over and turned off the recorder.

"I witnessed you murder Alan Chambers. We have the murder weapon with your fingerprints on it and CCTV footage that clearly documents the incident. You have been charged with murder and you will go to prison for maybe twenty years. What I can't understand is why you were in Hackney, and why did you attack an innocent man on his way home from a long day at work?" Star asked.

"He was not that innocent," Ty said.

"What do you mean by that? Did he hurt you?"

Ty laughed out loud and shook his head.

"A snotty nosed middle-class accountant hurt me? Not a chance," Ty said as he lounged back in his chair and put his hands behind his head.

"How did you know he was an accountant?"

Star immediately saw the look of shock in his eyes

"No comment," Ty said as he returned to sitting behind the desk.

"You knew him, didn't you? Maybe you did some business together which went wrong. Did he steal from you?"

"No comment," Ty said firmly.

"There's no tape recorder on here, Ty. I'm just trying to understand why you did it."

"We all pay the price for our deeds, Five-O, even you. Now I've got no more to say until I see my solicitor," Ty said, and slowly turned his head away.

"Officer, take this man back to his cell," Star said as she stood up. She reached down for her file and began to walk towards the door. She turned.

"I will get to the bottom of this. You're hiding something, but I'm on to you," Star said.

Ty turned abruptly.

"I know who you are, and I can find out where you live, who your friends are, your family and those you love. Don't push too hard Five-O, or you will suffer unimaginable pain," Ty said as he glared at Star.

"Send who you like Ty and I'll put them on their back just like I did you," Star replied as she stepped out into the hallway.

"Why, you!" Ty yelled as he stood up and sent the wooden chair over backwards and onto the floor.

Chapter 3

Great Queen Street London WC2, United Grand Lodge of England.

The Masonic Brotherhood is a group of people, a society, with secrets. An estimated twenty percent of the quarter of a million UK lodge members are high ranking police officers while other active brethren include politicians, senior military officers, bankers, lawyers, judges and leading businessmen. They have an on-going reputation of banding together to help each other. Freemasons come from all faiths and backgrounds. Freemasons believe in a 'Supreme Being' and think very highly of other free and accepted masons, and therefore consider helping them in their careers or businesses to be of mutual benefit. In the not-too-distant past, laws have been broken to effectively benefit the brotherhood.

Freemasonry is probably the most powerful society on earth.

Detective Inspector Ronald Pratt was a career police officer. He shared his time between the police force and his masonic duties. Ronald had not been fortunate with relationships and chose to stay at the family home to care for his mother after his father, a senior police officer and Freemason, passed away suddenly. His father had introduced Ronald to the world of freemasonry shortly after the failure of his second long term relationship. Almost immediately he felt at home alongside the men in dark suits, black shoes, white shirts, black ties, white gloves, aprons and regalia. It provided him with a sense of belonging, a direction and an environment where he could learn, apply what he had learned, and progress with like-minded men. Ronald had never been popular socially or with his work colleagues.

Having concluded a successful criminal operation, for example, all the team members would celebrate at a pub. Ronald was often overlooked and on the rare occasion he did attend, he felt that he didn't fit in and would slip away unnoticed. However, armed with a handshake which allowed other Freemasons to recognise him, his rank, and standing in the lodge, the promotional opportunities began to present themselves to him and consequently he moved up in the force. Behind the closed doors of a Masonic lodge, only your rank within the craft carried any power, weight or influence. Ronald had moved through the offices by consistently impressing those around him with his dedication and loyalty to the craft and his fellow brethren. Outside the lodge, Ronald was a Detective Inspector and answerable to a number of ranks above him. Inside the lodge he was the all-powerful worshipful master supported by decades of worldly wise and powerful past masters.

Ronald put his black briefcase on the table. He opened it and reached inside for his white gloves, masonic apron, regalia and Jewel of Office.

"Good evening, Worshipful Master," a fellow mason greeted him.

"Good evening, Brother," Ronald said, as he clipped on his apron.

"It's exciting, a third degree raising, Worshipful Master. It should be a very good evening," said another brother.

A traditional lodge will only accept one or two entered apprentice, first degree Freemasons during any one year. They will be taught the secrets applicable to their degree. The entered apprentice will then pass on to become a fellowcraft, and then finally to the highest rank of a Master Mason.

Wearing his apron and regalia, Ronald confidently entered the temple which is always orientated east to west. It was a rectangular room with seats around the perimeter, so all the brothers had a good view of the proceedings. Ronald looked at the altar situated in the middle of the room. He was pleased to see the volume of sacred law had been placed on it with three lighted candles set in a triangle as a reminder of the compass. Ronald watched as the Inner-Guard, and Junior and Senior Deacon took their positions. He looked over at both his Junior and Senior wardens. Happy that everyone was in their correct place he moved over and took up his supreme position in the Worshipful Master's chair. He turned to his left and smiled at the Chaplain before glancing over and acknowledging the immediate past Master on his right.

Worshipful Master Ronald Pratt instructed that the lodge be opened in the third degree. The lodge went quiet as a series of knocks were made on the door. The Inner-Guard stood up in front of his chair at the North of the Senior Warden. He took a step forward and gave the secret sign of the Third Degree which he held until instructed by the Junior Warden.

"Brother Junior Warden, there is a report."

The Junior Warden stood up, took a step forward and gave the sign to the Worshipful Master which he held until instructed by Ronald.

"Worshipful Master there is a report," said the Junior Warden.

"Brother Junior Warden enquire who wants admission."

The Inner-Guard followed the black-and-white square tiled floor until he reached the door.

"Who have you there?"

"Brother Jonathan Pierce, who has been regularly initiated into Freemasonry, passed to the degree of Fellowcraft and has made such progress as he hopes will entitle him to be raised to the sublime Degree of Master Mason for which ceremony he has been properly prepared," said the Tyler.

The Inner-Guard checked to see that the candidate was properly prepared.

"How does he hope to obtain the privileges of the Third Degree?"

"By the help of God, the united aid of the square and compass and the benefit of a password," said the Tyler.

"Is he in possession of the password?" said the Inner-Guard.

"Will you prove him?" said the Tyler.

The Inner-Guard extended his right hand and the candidate, with the instruction of the Tyler, gave him a pass grip and password leading from the second to the third degree.

"Halt while I report to the Worshipful Master," the Inner-Guard said as he closed the door. He then returned to his chair at the North of the Senior Warden.

"Worshipful Master, Brother Jonathan Pierce who has been regularly initiated into Freemasonry passed to the Degree of Fellowcraft and has made such further progress that he hopes will entitle him to be raised to the sublime Degree of Master Mason for which he is properly prepared."

"How does he hope to obtain the privileges of The Third Degree?" Ronald asked.

"By the help of God, the united aid of the square and compass and the benefit of a password," the Inner-Guard replied.

"We acknowledge the powerful aid by which he seeks admission. Do you, Brother Inner-Guard, vouch that he is in possession of the password?" Ronald said.

"I do, Worshipful Master."

"Then let him be admitted in due form," said Robert as he nodded towards his officers. "Brother Deacons."

The Inner-Guard and both Deacons proceeded to the door of the lodge. The Junior Deacon, en-route, placed a kneeling stool on the floor. The Senior Deacon placed himself at a position by the door so that he could take the candidate by the right hand on admission to the Lodge. The Inner-Guard opened the door. He had in his hand a compass that was widely extended. He presented one point simultaneously on each breast and then raised the compass above his head to signify that he had done so. The Senior Deacon took the candidate by the right hand and led him to the kneeling stool. The Junior Deacon took up his position on the candidate's left.

"Advance as a Fellowcraft, first as an Apprentice," the Senior Deacon said.

The candidate took a step and gave the sign of an entered apprentice freemason. He then took a second step and gave the sign of the Fellowcraft.

"Let the candidate kneel while the blessing of Heaven is invoked on what we are about to do," Ronald said.

The remainder of the ceremony passed with the candidate being raised from Fellowcraft to the sublime Degree of Master Mason.

It was customary for the brethren to share a meal and wine together after all Lodge meetings.

"Harry, how is that East London contract coming along?"

"We've had prices now from all the contractors, John. I'll give you a call on Monday so we can set up a date to go through your quotation."

"Thank you, Harry."

"Thomas, has the bank read through my business plan yet? I'll need that loan soon to complete the deal I have on that property in Chelsea with Brother Charles."

"Let Charles know it is just a formality. You'll have the money deposited in your account within the week."

"Thank you, Thomas."

"My son has just left University brother Thomas. Do you have any openings at your bank?"

"I'm sure we can find a suitable place for him. Ask him to contact me on Monday."

"Thank you, Brother Thomas."

As the evening came to a close, the Tyler stood up and raised his wine glass.

"To all poor and distressed Masons, wherever they may be, dispersed over the face of the earth or on the water, here's wishing them a relief from their sufferings, and a happy return to their native land should they so desire it."

"Worshipful Master, will you join me for a brandy upstairs in the lounge?" said Chief Superintendent Raymond Nichols.

"I would like that very much, Raymond," Ronald replied.

The two men bid their fellow brethren a good evening and left for the lounge bar. They sat back in their leather armchairs beside the roaring open fire.

"I have to formally congratulate you, Ronald, on your year as Worshipful Master. Freemasons throughout history have been taught morals and self-knowledge as they pass through each degree and office. Our allegorical plays follow ancient forms by using stone masons' customs and tools as allegorical guides and as you know I am a stickler for being word perfect and the rituals being strictly performed to the ancient rules and you, Worshipful Master, have excelled yourself. Well done!" Raymond said, as he raised his cut crystal brandy glass.

"Thank you, Raymond," Ronald said as the two brethren chinked glasses. "It's been an honour."

"You'll now pass to immediate past master and I've every confidence you will guide and direct the newly installed master to fulfil his obligations, responsibilities and perform his duties. The Craft has more in store for you, Ronald, but I'm not at liberty to discuss it with you until your year as the immediate past master concludes," Raymond said.

"You can be sure that the new worshipful master will perform ritual and degree work, pass on masonic knowledge and the science, morals, symbols and allegory to the best of my ability," Ronald said.

"I never doubted it. Anyway, how are you finding the front line and how is that sprightly young Detective Sergeant of yours?" Raymond asked.

"It's a daily battle out on the streets, sir, but we're making slow and solid progress. We've made another serious knife crime arrest. This time it's murder, a nasty business. Detective Sergeant Star Bellamy is making slow yet positive progression under my guidance. She can be a little frustrating at times, but I will knock her into the best shape I can to effectively do the job."

"Good, because we have bigger plans for you, Detective Inspector. I want you in that Detective Chief Inspector's role. Now, what I'm about to tell you can go no further, do you understand?" Raymond said, as he put his brandy glass back on the table and leant forward.

"Our view of governments is quite simple. They exist to fill the needs of the people, the real people who work, pay their bills and contribute to the economy. The role of a rightful government is to provide services that are for the good or benefit of those people as opposed to being on a profit basis. These services, if necessary and justified, are paid for through the tax system," Raymond said before letting out a sigh. "It grieves me to tell you Ronald, that the fascism of the Left has successfully infiltrated all levels of government, as well as the media and our education system."

There was a moment's silence as the enormity of the Chief Superintendent's words sank in.

"Do we know what the Left's agenda is?" Ronald asked.

"From what we can see, it's:

- The critical race theory
- Taxing the electorate beyond reason
- The dreaded white male is the source of all the world's problems
- Capitalism is unfair and racist
- The only thing that matters in the world is fighting climate change
- Open all the UK borders
- The police are evil
- Give social security payments in return for votes
- Indoctrination at schools to hate the United Kingdom
- Have no respect for the national flag
- Advocating that you get your news from social media
- Advocating that science is the answer to everything but insist that there are more than two biological genders.
- Promote Anti-Semitism towards Jews and Israel

The Left are pushing for more governmental control and despotism. The communists, fascists and socialists are taking power with the traditional ties being broken. There may come a time, Ronald, when we may have to fight for the very principles that the United Kingdom was founded on," Raymond said.

"Forgive me, but what is critical race theory?" Ronald asked.

"It's an academic movement which seeks to link race, racism and power. They challenge the very foundations of liberal order such as rationalism, constitutional law and legal reasoning. They believe that our social lives, political structures and economic systems are founded on race," Raymond said.

"What can I do? How can I help?" Ronald said as he leant further forward.

"Plans are being drawn up, Ronald. We have six million brethren worldwide with a reach into every city, town or village in the world. At the appropriate time, we will be ready to meet the challenge head on. For right now all I need to know is that you are with us and when the time comes, you will not falter and you will do your duty," Raymond said as he beckoned the waiter over to refill their glasses.

"I am with you brother. I will carry out my orders to the letter and without question," Ronald said.

Raymond sat forward and held out his hand for Ronald to shake.

"I knew that I could depend on you. Your father - my brother and my friend, would be very proud of you if he were here today. Well done!"

Chapter 4

It was just after 10.00am. Star had a couple of hours before she needed to get back for a meeting at the police station. She had lived in her two-bedroom apartment in Kensington, West London, for just over five years. Her mother, Jennifer, had left Star a sizeable inheritance which allowed her to buy the fully renovated luxurious apartment.

Jennifer Bellamy had passed suddenly while away in the United States. She had belonged to circle of powerful psychics. Jennifer had been born with extra sensory perception just as her mother had before. When she wasn't travelling, she would spend time with Star and tell her how the universe was brimming with unlimited and divine energy and that, in time, she could tap into it just as her mother had before her. Jennifer had taught Star how to concentrate and connect to its subtle vibrations. She had stressed the importance of the universal consciousness and the divine energy that ran through it and how every living thing was connected. With each year that passed, Star's gifts would not only become stronger, but she discovered new powers. Her gifts grew to incorporate clairsentience, the gift of being able to feel the same emotions of someone simply by touching them and psychometry, the ability to communicate with the deceased owner of an object. At twelve years of age, she received the gift of mediumship following the visit of a lost soul that needed a message relayed back to his wife. Jennifer had helped Star hone these gifts and had emphasised many times that there would come a time when she would be called to join the 'Pythia' just as she and the generations of women before her had.

Star had promised that she would visit and have tea with her elderly neighbour, Maude. She took her coat and bag and left her apartment.

She double locked the door after setting the alarm. She strolled down the marble tiled floor to Maude's home and pressed the doorbell. Moments later the door swung open.

"Yes?" said Tracey, the cleaner.

"Good morning, Tracey. Maude is expecting me," Star said as she stepped into the apartment and past Tracey.

"Well, you better come in then," Tracey said as she closed the door. "Oh, you already have."

"Is that you, Star?" Maude called out from the lounge.

Maude was in her late eighties. Her perfectly groomed hair was winter white, and her face was faded and timeworn, but her galaxy blue eyes lit up and twinkled like an earthshine pool.

"Hello Maude. I must say you are looking well. How is everything?"

Maude's smile was vivacious and captivating. It could instantly light up a room.

"I'm fine, Star, but I do worry about everything that's going on," Maude said. "Tracey, be a dear and make us a pot of tea, would you please?"

Star heard a heavy sigh from the kitchen.

"I don't know how you tolerate her behaviour," Star said shaking her head. "I have never met anyone quite as rude as her."

"I think that I might just be used to her now and I really don't want to make any trouble," Maude said.

"It's your home and she is your cleaner, so I suppose it's none of my business," Star replied.

Maude smiled awkwardly.

"So, what is it that you're worried about, Maude?" Star said as she turned back to face her elderly friend.

"I read the newspapers and scroll through the internet, and it feels like everyone is asleep because they're just not seeing what is happening in front of their eyes," said Maude. "I think that IQ's must have dropped sharply in the last ten to twenty years because people are acting like sheep and just doing or believing whatever they're being told."

"Do you not think that society has always been like that though Maude?" Star asked.

Tracey brought a pot of tea with cups and saucers in on a tray. She put them on the coffee table.

"It's the New World Order, Star. They are slowly and secretly generating a totalitarian world government," Maude said, as she reached forward and began to stir the tea pot.

Star looked up as Tracey tutted loudly and rolled her eyes.

"Thank you for the tea, Tracey. Don't let us keep you," Star said.

Tracey's nose scrunched up and her face became contorted with bitter resentment. She shot Star a dirty look, spun around and stomped out of the room, muttering under her breath.

Tracey had known Maude through a friend of a friend, and when she fell on hard times Maude offered Tracey a job cleaning her apartment and running a few errands on her behalf. Maude had paid Tracey twice the market rate. At first she had been grateful for the opportunity to get back on her feet with an income. However, the gratitude soon turned to resentment. Tracey had never been a truly optimistic person and had no interest in turning the sour hand life had dealt her into a sweeter one. She had always struggled to see the silver lining. Life had dealt her one bitter and jaded blow too many and increasingly she became embittered, held grudges, was jealous of those around her and found herself focusing on the darker side of life. Star had come across jealous, vindictive people in her career both in the police force and while dealing with criminals, but Tracey was by far the worst. Initially Star had tried to be friendly but the nasty, jealous, cutting comments and sweeping statements that were delivered by Tracey made her difficult to like or get on with. She was unpleasant company and in the early days her persistent negativity began to have an effect on Star. There were days when Star would stand outside Maude's front door and hesitate to knock as a feeling of dread washed over her entire body. Star came to the same conclusion as Maude. There was not much a person could do to help someone so bitter. Tracey was angry with everyone, everywhere and only she could help herself. To Star, Tracey was irrelevant and believed that Maude deserved a medal from Her Majesty the Queen for her patience and understanding.

"I'm telling you Star. The secretive power elite have a globalist agenda and they're conspiring to eventually rule the world through an authoritarian one world government. I truly believe that they will replace sovereign national states. I'm a lot older than you, Star, and in all my years I have never witnessed so much division in the world. Families, friends and work colleagues falling out over opinions, ideologies or beliefs. In my day we just accepted that everyone had a democratic right to have their opinion. We didn't have to agree with it, but we accepted that they were entitled to it through the sacrifices made by the lives of our forefathers. It's the oldest and most effective strategy in all of history to divide the masses and conquer," Maude said as she poured the Earl Grey tea into the bone china cups.

Tracey let out a loud, fake, laugh in the hallway.

"The world is very definitely in a state of change right now but maybe, just maybe, it has always been that way. Back in your day, Maude, all you had was a daily newspaper and the news on television. Both were very selective with what was reported. Newspapers need to attract readers to sell advertising, so they opt for something headline grabbing and sensationalist and the news on television is limited by the amount of time that has been allocated. Today, if you chose, you could spend all day on the internet researching something that has no trusted sources and unqualified people are just airing their views online because, well, because they want to be famous," Star said.

"I told her a hundred times over not to spend all her time on the internet following conspiracy theories or they'd be locking her up," Tracey called out from the hallway.

Star shot up from her chair.

"Please, Star, just leave it," said Maude.

Star took a deep breath and sat back down.

"If what you're saying is true, Maude, how would it impact you? How do you think it would affect your life here in Kensington?" Star said before taking a sip from her cup.

"The most powerful men on the planet have no empathy for the people, Star. With a rising population, almost eight billion, drawing from a finite number of resources, we are all ripe for a cull. The new world order will want to depopulate the world to a more manageable five hundred million, maybe two billion at the most. They could do this through creating hatred, dehumanising races of people, like the Nazi's did in World War Two or unsustainable, exploitive, international development which leads to hunger, starvation and famine. Failing that, the creation and spread of an infectious disease leading to a global pandemic," Maude said.

"Bloody ridiculous," Tracey called out.

"Maude, can I suggest you try to get out more and not worry yourself with things that none of us can control?" Star said in a lowered tone as she stood up and kissed Maude on the cheek. "I have an important meeting at work, so I have to go."

"Off you trot then," Tracey called out.

"If you ever decide that you want a cleaner that just gets on with her duties without voicing their unwanted opinions, let me know," Star said with a wry smile.

"Will you come again?" said Maude.

"Of course, maybe we could catch a show in the West End one night," Star said.

"How about one of our afternoon tea sessions at Claridges," Maude said with a broad smile. "It feels like it's been months since we last went and it would be fun."

"I'll call today to try and make a reservation," Star said.

"Oh, goody," Maude said happily as she rubbed her frail hands together.

"I'll see myself out, Maude. You have a good day," Star said.

***

Star left and got into her black Range Rover Sport. As she turned the ignition key the engine fired up. *'Against All Odds by Phil Collins'* boomed out of the speakers. She reached over and turned the CD player off. The Phil Collins Greatest Hits album had been her mother's favourite and she would play it over and over when she wasn't travelling for the 'Circle'. She slipped the automatic gear shifter into drive and pulled out of the car park and onto the main road. Star was parking her car in the police car park just twenty minutes later. As she got out of the car, she felt a familiar shiver pass through her. Her chest tightened and there, before her, was the apparition of the old woman she had encountered on the night of Alan Chambers murder.

"Justice, get me justice for my son. Lauren is not what she seems!"

The apparition faded away.

"Who is Lauren?" Star thought as she locked her car door.

Once inside the police station, Detective Sergeant Star Bellamy met with the team.

"DI Pratt has called in to say he won't be here, DS Bellamy, and that he wants us to dot the I's and cross the T's and get ready to move on," Detective Constable Robin Carpenter said.

"Thank you, Robin," Star said as she stood by the large white board at the front of the room. She looked around at the team of four.

"Right, what did you find out, Robin?"

"I called into Mr Chamber's place of work. They were shocked but did just happen to let it slip that he was under investigation. They had nothing to conclusively prove his guilt, but a large number of fake invoices had been passed for payment totalling around £657,000. I spoke with a friend of his," DC Robin Carpenter said, as he flicked through his notes, "a Mr Michael Grant. He said that Mr Chambers had confided in him that his wife, Lauren Chambers, was suffering from a rare disease that could only be cured by some doctor in America. It sounded suspicious so I asked DC Sally York to find out what she could about Mrs Lauren Chambers."

Star felt the hairs on the back of her neck rise when she heard the name Lauren.

"What did you find out Sally?"

"The couple had been married for just over two years. They met through an online dating agency. Mrs Lauren Chambers had been married before to an accountant, a Mr Andrew West. He worked in the city," DC Sally York said.

"I called Mr Andrew West's place of work. Apparently, there was an internal investigation into a large sum of money that had gone missing. The investigation came to a halt after Mr Andrew West became the victim of a hit and run motoring accident. My contact there asked if Lauren West had been cured."

"I dug a little deeper too," said DC Sally York. "Before she became Mrs Lauren West, she was Lauren Brown. She was born in Croydon's Mayday Hospital and lived in the same road as Ty Patterson. I managed to track them both back to the same class in school."

"Good work Robin, thank you Sally. Okay, it looks like Mrs Lauren Chambers is a possible suspect in a conspiracy to murder both Alan Chambers and Andrew West. She had the opportunity, motive and the means. Both men were accountants and had access to large sums of money, which gave Lauren the opportunity. The motive was money, and the means was her school friend Mr Ty Patterson, the leader of a notorious bloody and violent postcode gang. Where is Ty Patterson now?"

"He was taken to court this morning and remanded in custody. They took him to Brixton Prison," DC Robin Carpenter said.

"Okay, we need to bring Mrs Chambers in. Tell her it's just routine. Can you and Sally do that?" Star said as she nodded at DC Robin Carpenter.

"Yes, DS Bellamy," DC Robin Carpenter said.

Sally smiled and nodded.

Star picked up the telephone and called HM Brixton prison to arrange to see Ty Patterson, and then drove over to South London. She parked in the car park and approached the gate. Star presented her warrant card and the prison officer confirmed she was expected, albeit at short notice. The Gate Officer asked for her mobile phone. An officer was assigned to stay with her while she moved around the jail to the interview room. Star sat down. Moments later Ty Patterson was led through the door.

"Good afternoon, Ty. You may remember me. I'm Detective Sergeant Star Bellamy. Please take a seat."

Star took out a packet of cigarettes and put them in the middle of the table.

"I understand that you were advised of your right to consult a legal advisor before this interview but have declined," Star said, as she pushed the pack of cigarettes towards him.

Ty grunted and nodded.

"Ty, did you know the victim, Alan Chambers?" Star said as she leant back in the wooden chair.

Ty shrugged his shoulders and shook his head before lighting a cigarette and placing the pack in front of him.

"Did you know his wife, Lauren Chambers?"

Star watched as his demeanour quickly changed.

"Nah," Ty said finally.

"You see, I find that interesting because Mrs Chambers, who was previously Mrs West and whose maiden name was Lauren Brown has said differently," Star said, as she watched Ty's body language.

"I don't know her," Ty said, as drew heavily on the cigarette.

"So, it's not the same Lauren Brown that you went to school with or the same girl who lived just a few doors down from your parent's home?" said Star.

Ty stiffened, almost imperceptibly.

"Did you know a Mr Andrew West, Lauren's previous husband?" Star said as she slowly leant forward.

"I know bags of people, but I don't know him!" Ty said adamantly.

"Did you know that Mr Andrew West was the victim of a hit and run?"

"Don't know him," Ty said.

"Did you know that Mr Andrew West was under investigation for the mishandling of a large sum of money? Several hundred thousand pounds I believe," Star said.

Star watched as Ty's eyes lit up when she mentioned the large sum of money.

"Alan Chambers was also being investigated for the loss of almost three quarters of a million pounds. Did you know that?"

Star could see her comments were having an effect.

"Mrs Lauren Chambers has said she knows you, Ty. She knows you to be the leader of a fierce and violent gang," Star said. "Why do you think she would come into the police station and tell us about you and her?"

Ty remained quiet.

"Lauren's late husbands are suspected of fraudulently taking over one million pounds Ty. Let me just say that again. One million pounds. Lauren alleged that you were jealous of both Mr Andrew West and Mr

Alan Chambers. Is that true, Ty? Were you jealous or was it just about the money?" said Star.

"She got over a million quid?"

Star nodded.

"Was she planning on sharing that with you, Ty? Was it a first love kind of thing and the money would give you both a better life?"

"A million fucking quid!" Ty yelled.

Star nodded.

"Can I tell you what I think happened?" Star said.

Ty said nothing. He was still muttering 'a million quid' over and over, shaking his head.

"I believe Lauren was right and you have known each other since your schooldays. I think Lauren told you something about Mr Andrew West that made you angry. Maybe that he was violent or was mistreating her. Does that sound right?"

Ty was still muttering over and over, 'a million quid'.

"I believe she contacted you again after she married Mr Alan Chambers. I think that she gave you a similar story, only this time she offered to pay you to 'take care' of Mr Chambers. Lauren is a very convincing witness, Ty, and I can only imagine that two or three hundred thousand pounds would have been a life changing amount of money for you and another knife crime victim in the capital would just be another statistic. You would have been home free to spend all that lovely money in any way you chose."

"One million quid, the bitch!" Ty shrieked.

"Is there something you want to share with me Ty? Is there something that you can tell me that will help me to ask the courts to be more lenient with you. As we sit here today, Ty, you are looking at life imprisonment. You'll be out in twenty-five years, if you're lucky," said Star.

"What can you do for me?"

"The best that I can do is advise the judge that you were co-operative in bringing the true guilty party to justice," said Star.

"Not good enough. I need something in writing, a pardon in return for the truth," Ty said as he stubbed his cigarette out and immediately lit another.

"There are officers that would lie to you, Ty, and say that can happen. The truth is, the best any officer can do is speak directly to the judge and formally acknowledge that you helped bring the investigation to its correct conclusion. The judge will then do what judges do and use his judgement," Star said.

"Do I have your word?" Ty said, as he looked up and stared deep into Star's eyes.

"You have my word that once you have made a police statement I will speak to the judge on your behalf," Star said meeting his gaze head on.

"Okay," Ty said as he exhaled the cigarette smoke and blew it up towards the ceiling.

"Whenever you're ready," Star said.

Ty took a second deep drag on his cigarette.

"Yeah, I know Lauren. She was a wifey from way back in the day. We lost contact after she moved away from Croydon and then one day, from out of nowhere, she came back and found me. Lauren was still lush and seeing her again was safe and we were meshing like back in the day. She told me that she'd got with some tourist who was beating on her. She asked me to get her a mash so she could take care of him. I was vexed, so I said I'd take care of it," Ty said.

"Okay, Ty, just so I haven't missed anything with the London slang, I'll repeat what I understand you have just said," Star said.

Ty nodded.

"You have known Lauren since your school days and at one point she was your girlfriend. She went away and then returned. You found her to still be good looking and within a short period of time you became lovers. Lauren told you she was married to a 'clueless person' is that correct?"

Ty nodded.

"He was abusive, so she asked you to get her a gun so that she could take care of him."

Ty nodded again.

"You were clearly very angry and said you would kill Mr Andrew West, the man you believed was physically beating your friend and lover, on her behalf. Is that correct?"

Ty Nodded.

"I wasn't going to shoot him; it would bring down too much heat from the Feds so I hoisted a car and waited in the place Lauren said he would be at. I had a photo, so when I saw him I just ran the mother fucker over. I was vexed, you know. Lauren said he would take his belt to her. He needed to pay. She said the Po-Po would be asking questions, so we stayed apart," said Ty.

"So, you stole a car and because you believed that Mr Andrew West had been physically abusing Lauren, you were angry, and so having checked it was him from the photograph provided by Lauren West you proceeded to run him down at high speed. Lauren was then concerned that the police would be investigating the incident and so you stayed apart. Is that correct?"

Ty Nodded.

"Lauren just stayed away. I didn't know where to contact her and another few years passed before she returned to Croydon. It was just like before, only this time she offered me eight thousand pounds to have him hanging with Elvis," Ty said.

"Did you become lovers again?" said Star

Ty nodded his head slowly.

"I was vexed that Lauren didn't come back to me and had married another man with anger issues. I took the money even though Lauren said this time she would move back to Croydon and we would be together. I wanted to believe her and part of me still does," Ty said. "The rest you know. Knifing him seemed the obvious way to take care of him. With a knife related street murder every day, it's like you said, just another number for your bean counters. I didn't count on you being around," said Ty. "That bitch not once said anything about a million quid. I've been 'owned' Five-O, but I ain't taking it lying down. I should have been given half of that stash at least. The bitch has turned me over and she has to pay with silver or blood."

"For absolute clarity, Ty, are you are telling me that Lauren instigated and was party to both the murder of Mr Andrew West and Mr Alan Chambers?"

"For sure!" Ty said, as he sat back in the chair and crossed his arms.

"Thank you, Ty. I will now ask one of my officers to meet with you and take an official police statement. Are you happy for me to do that?"

Ty nodded vehemently.

"Thank you. In return I will keep my promise and speak to the judge when the case goes to court," said Star.

"What kind of reduced sentence do you think I'll get. Ten years? I could be out in five with good behaviour. I could do five years easy," Ty said, as he lit another cigarette.

"I don't know," Star said, shaking her head, "But the court will look favourably on you for co-operating. I hope you only get the ten years you feel you deserve."

Ty held the cigarettes up in his hand.

"Keep them," said Star. "I don't smoke."

Chapter 5

Star was at home in her apartment. It was just after 9.00 pm when she climbed out of the Radox filled bath she had run for herself an hour before. As she dried herself, she called out to Alexa, the Amazon virtual assistant. The Alexa device was built for voice recognition.

"Alexa," Star called out as she slipped into her dressing gown. "Play *'One More Night'* by Phil Collins."

There was a ping sound before Alexa sourced and played the Phil Collins hit.

Star slumped back into her armchair before reaching for her half full glass of red wine. She took a sip and then looked up Julia's telephone number.

"Hello, is that you Star?" Julia said

"Hi Julia, how are you?"

"Everything was just so-so until you called,"

Star smiled "That's a nice thing to say."

"You're a nice person to say it to," Julia replied.

"Thank you."

"What kind of a day have you had?" Julia asked.

"Very satisfying actually," Star said.

"I'm pleased to hear that." Julia said. "Are you on your way out?"

"No, I've been home about an hour or so and have just got out of a steaming hot bath," Star said. "I'm feeling relaxed, chilled and have poured myself a large glass of red wine," Star said.

"That sounds wonderful.," Julia replied. "I can't think of a better way to end a day except maybe sharing that glass of red wine or even the bath with a special someone."

"You are naughty, Julia."

"I can be."

"What are you doing on Saturday night?" Star asked.

"It's lucky you finished that last sentence with 'on Saturday night' or you would have found out just how naughty I can be," Julia replied cheekily

Star giggled.

"I was hoping to see this amazingly attractive police officer I'd met recently," Julia said.

"You're making me blush."

"You have no idea how much I'd like to make you do that," Julia said.

Star chuckled.

"So will you come out with me on Saturday?" Star asked.

"I can't think of anything else I'd rather do."

"Then it's a date. I'll make reservations at a wonderful little Italian restaurant I know and will text you the details."

"That sounds perfect," Julia said. "Shall I bring an overnight bag?"

Both the girls began to chuckle.

"You have a good evening and I'll see you on Saturday," Star said

"You too, Star."

Star ended the call. She sat back in her chair and grinned. As she reached over for her glass of wine her mobile phone pinged. It was a text message from Julia. It read:

'How did you get to be so irresistibly gorgeous?'

Star chuckled to herself and then messaged back.

'Maybe I was born this way………. Not!'

Star swallowed the last of her wine and then refilled the glass. Her phone pinged again. She opened the message to find a picture of Julia in a strawberry red negligee. She was holding out her open hand, palm up, in front of her ruby red lips and blowing a kiss. Star couldn't help thinking how sexy and alluring Julia looked in the photo and began to imagine how Saturday night could go. As she lay back and allowed her imagination to drift, she opened her eyes and sat bolt upright as the temperature in the room began to fall. She could hear the familiar high-pitched sound in her ear as her chest tightened. The lamp light began to flicker as the fourth of Phil Collin's greatest hits began to stutter. In the far corner of the room a translucent image of a soldier began to appear. Star clambered off the chair and onto her feet. As an empath and medium, Star had porous energy fields and was open to earth bound spirits. She immediately crossed her arms over her chakra energy point. The spirit of the soldier flickered.

"Help me. I was murdered."

"No, not now! I am busy. Leave my home now!" Star commanded.

The spirit faded away, the lamp flickered back on, and Alexa played *'Another Day in Paradise'* by Phil Collins.

"Damn, sometimes I just wish the dead would leave me alone," thought Star.

Shortly after Star's twelfth birthday she was in her bedroom and was woken by the spirit of a young girl asking for her help. Star's mother, Jennifer, had been coaching her in preparation for when the first earth bound spirit sought her help. It was unlike anything she had imagined. The young girl looked so helpless, so lost. Jennifer had told her how some of the deceased remain on the earth's plane after their physical body dies. Star was quick to learn that these spirits could still feel the emotions of pain, anger and frustration. The young girl, Emma, couldn't understand she was dead and called out for her mother. Star overcame her fear, calmed herself, and spoke with the spirit. She told Emma that she should have moved on to the astral realm and that her spirit guide would find her and lead her into the light. Emma visited for three consecutive nights. Star had learnt that her family had been in a horrific car accident. On the fourth night a second ghostly image materialised at the end of her bed. It was a bright, white, light in the outline of a human form. Emma, the spirit, called out 'mummy, mummy' and edged towards the light. Then as quickly as the bright white light appeared, it vanished, with Emma.

Like all young psychics, Star questioned what was wrong with her and asked why she had been cursed with these gifts. As her powers developed, Star felt an overwhelming sense of guilt after a tragic event took place that she instinctively knew was going to happen but hadn't done anything about it. She experienced a roller coaster of emotion with each individual encounter. Emma was the first of many seeking Star's help.

Jennifer was insistent that Star was not to share the knowledge her mother was passing on, or reveal the gifts that had been bestowed upon her. She emphasised that people, as a rule, are quick to judge and the church and those that blindly follow the words that have been written, translated and rewritten by man, will label anything that cannot be explained as evil. Star had been quick to understand, having read the works of Karl Marx, that mainstream religions were constructed by people to calm uncertainty over their role in the universe and society.

Star poured the last few drops of red wine down the sink. She was feeling tired, it had been a long day and the Radox bath and confirmation that she would be meeting with Julia on Saturday had both excited and relaxed her. At just after 11.00 pm Star went to bed.

Chapter 6

"Detective Sergeant Bellamy, we have brought Mrs Lauren Chambers in and placed her in the interview room," DC Robin Carpenter said.

"How is she?"

"We did exactly what you said, Sergeant. She believes she's here to help fill in some missing information."

"Excellent. I'd like you and DC Sally York to visit Ty Patterson at HMP Brixton. He's keen to make a statement. Can you do that for me, please?"

"Yes, Sergeant. I'll call ahead and get that tied up for you this afternoon."

"Good job, Robin. Thank you." Star said, as she picked up a brown card folder and pen from her desk.

Just as Robin left her office Detective Inspector Pratt stepped in.

"Sir," Star said as she clambered to her feet.

"Right, what's the status on the Chambers' murder?" DI Pratt said as he strolled in and sat down.

Star couldn't help noticing he was wearing the same suit with the soup stain on the left collar. He was in need of a full shave that included having his nasal and ear hair removed.

"There have been a number of developments, sir."

Star went on to explain the outcome of her visit to Ty Patterson at HMP Brixton and that both DC Robin Carpenter and DC Sally York were on their way to obtain a statement that implicated Mrs Lauren Chambers as a conspirator to both the murder of her previous husband, Mr Andrew West, and Mr Alan Chambers. The Inspector's eyes lit up.

"We need to bring her in, Bellamy." DI Pratt said as he jumped to his feet.

"She's already here, sir. In the interview room,"

"Good, right. Now I want you to demonstrate all the things that I've trained you in," DI Pratt said as he strode towards the door.

"You trained me in! You're pretty damn useless, a relic of a bygone age that should have been retired off years ago. You, sir, are a Pratt by name and a Pratt by nature," thought Star.

"Yes sir, I will," Star said as she followed him out of the office and down to the interview rooms.

They stopped outside the interview room.

"Now remember Detective Sergeant Bellamy, just as I've trained you," DI Pratt said.

"Twat!" thought Star.

Star opened the interview door and entered the room. Lauren was holding a cigarette and standing behind the desk. She looked over at Star and smiled. She had a slim, sculptured figure with a tapered waist. Her skin was perfect, and her complexion had a citron tint. Her hair was ore-gold, bright and luxurious. Star could see instantly how men and women, if they were that way inclined, could fall for her easily.

"Please, take a seat," Star said as she motioned her towards the wooden chair. "I am Detective Sergeant Star Bellamy, and this is Detective Inspector Ronald Pratt."

"Thank you," Lauren said as she sat down and pulled the chair closer to the desk.

Star placed the folder in front of her.

"I'd like to thank you for coming in today. I appreciate this must be a very difficult time for you," said Star.

Lauren nodded.

"You just don't expect this kind of thing to happen to somebody you know, let alone your husband," Lauren said.

"How long were you married to Mr Chambers, Lauren?"

"Almost three years. The time has passed so quickly," said Lauren.

"Do you have any children or dependents?"

Lauren shook her head.

"We often spoke about starting a family, but Alan was always so busy at work," Lauren said.

"I imagine with Alan working in finance in such a large corporation, your time together must have been limited," Star said.

"We had weekends and Alan would try to surprise me with special nights out or weekends away," Lauren replied.

"Did Alan seem stressed or under any kind of pressure from either work or maybe something from outside of work?" said Star.

Lauren shook her head.

"Not really. I mean there were always deadlines to meet but there wasn't anything that I hadn't seen before," Lauren said as she relaxed back into the chair.

"So, is there anything you can think of that would have resulted in your husband being brutally murdered?" Star said as she fingered the corner of the folder.

"No," Lauren said as she shook her head. "I couldn't imagine anyone wanting to hurt Alan."

A single tear rolled down Lauren's cheek. Star reached into her pocket and produced a small packet of tissues. She opened the pack and handed Lauren one.

"Thank you. I still can't believe he's gone. I'm sorry." Lauren said.

"No problem, Lauren, take your time."

"Thank you," Lauren said wiping away the tear.

"Does the name Ty Patterson mean anything to you, Lauren?"

Star spotted an immediate change in Lauren's composure.

"Err, no, I don't think so," Lauren stuttered.

"Take some time and try to recall that name if you can," Star said.

Star watched as Lauren placed her Aphrodite-red fingernails on her acorn cup chin.

"No, that name doesn't ring any bells. Why, should it?" Lauren said finally.

Star opened her folder and used her index finger to scroll down the handwritten notes.

"Did you not go to school with a Ty Patterson?"

"I may have done, but school was a long time ago. I may not remember," Lauren said.

"Are you suffering from any kind of illness Lauren?"

"No, maybe a little traumatised by the death of my husband," said Lauren.

"Do you know why one of your husband's work colleagues would think you were suffering from a rare medical condition and that only an operation in the United States could save your life?" Star asked as she ran her finger back over the handwritten notes.

"No, no. I have no idea what would make a person say something like that," Lauren said, shaking her head vehemently.

"Were you aware that your husband was under investigation at work for misappropriation of funds?" Star said, as she turned the page over.

"No, that's the first I've heard of it," Lauren said.

"Your first husband, Mr Andrew West, he was an accountant, wasn't he?"

Lauren could not disguise her look of shock when her late husband's name was mentioned.

"Yes, he was." Lauren said eventually.

"Did you know that *he* was being investigated after the sum of £657,000 was discovered missing," said Star.

"I didn't know anything about that," Lauren said.

"When we spoke to a former colleague of Mr West he asked after you and hoped you had received the medical help you needed. Why do you think he would say that?" said Star.

"I have no idea where any of this is coming from!" Lauren said.

"Lauren, please think very carefully before answering this next question," Star said.

"Okay," Lauren replied.

"We have arrested Mr Ty Patterson for the murder of your husband Mr Alan Chambers," said Star.

"Thank goodness, well done!" said Lauren with a sigh of relief.

"When I interviewed Ty in prison, he made some shocking claims which I'm hoping you'll be able to help us with."

Lauren remained silent. Star watched as the blood drained from her face.

"Ty Patterson confessed to murdering your first husband, Andrew West. He claimed you were lovers and that you tried to buy a gun from him to protect yourself from abusive behaviours," Star said.

Lauren remained silent.

"He also said you paid him eight thousand pounds to murder your husband, Alan Chambers. How would you like to respond to that?"

Lauren remained silent for a few moments.

"Oh my God, I'm so pleased it's safe for me to finally talk and tell the truth. Yes, I've known Ty Patterson since we were children together in Croydon. We had an intense and volatile relationship. Ty would never take no for answer. It was unhealthy and became harmful and destructive to my physical, mental and emotional well-being. Whilst Ty would never actually physically attack me, he became extremely controlling. He would tell me what I could and couldn't wear out. He would insist on knowing where I was at all times and who I was with. He would say over and over that it was only because he loved me so much that he acted that way. I felt under pressure to do as he bid. He manipulated me. I cannot stress how much psychological pressure that put on me. I was under his control, under the control of a bloody, violent gang leader who even the police were scared to tackle. As the relationship became increasingly volatile, I suddenly came to my senses and decided to get out, get away from Ty and the area I grew up in," Lauren said.

"So you escaped. What happened next?"

"I met the most wonderful man, Andy; he was everything that Ty wasn't. Hard working, with a good job and he loved me. It was then that Ty found me. I don't know how, but he found me. He said that if I didn't give him money he would kill Andy, my Andy. I pretended to have an illness that needed expensive treatment in the US. Andy exhausted all his lines of credit and then did something at work. You have to understand that he thought I was dying so what he did was out of character. He gave me the money to hide away in case the investigation turned on him. I gave everything to Ty, thousands of pounds, to keep Andy safe. Then Ty, for whatever reason, killed Andy anyway," Lauren said as the tears streamed down her face.

Star handed her a second tissue.

"I couldn't go to the police. I just knew I had to run, which was what I did. It was then that I met Alan; he was sweet, loving and kind. I thought that at least I could have the kind of life that I'd previously only dreamed of. But it wasn't long before Ty found me again. He threatened to kill Alan if I didn't pay him just as before, and so the whole cycle started again. I hoped and prayed that Ty would just take the money and leave us alone. But, oh no, he wasn't going to allow me to be happy, so he killed Alan."

"Thank you for opening up and sharing that harrowing story with us," DI Pratt said. "It would help us to clear all this nasty business up if you could make a statement with everything you've just told us. Can you do that for us?"

"Yes, of course. I'm just so pleased that it's all in the open now and with Ty Patterson in prison I'll be safe to get on with my life," Lauren said.

DI Ronald Pratt smiled and nodded before standing up and beckoning Star to leave the room with him. When they were both outside in the hallway DI Pratt closed the door shut firmly.

"Right, we have her bang to rights now. Get a statement Detective Sergeant, and make sure she includes everything that's just been shared with us. Then I want you to run what you have by the CPS solicitor and then charge them both," whispered DI Pratt.

"Yes sir," said Star.

"We should both be patting ourselves on the back for this one, don't you think?" DI Pratt said as he straightened himself up to stand over Star.

"Yes, sir. Thank you, sir," Star said.

"One of these days you will be exposed for the imposter you are. Your lack of integrity in taking credit for my good police work is just another example of your unprincipled behaviour. I'll toe the line and play the game, but your days are numbered, Pratt!" thought Star. *"You will slip up and I'll be there to see you fall."*

Following advice form the Crown Prosecution, formal charges were raised against both Mrs Lauren Chambers and Mr Ty Patterson. Star had a final visit from the apparition who had asked for justice. Star told her that justice would be forthcoming and that she should move back into the light to be with her son, Alan Chambers.

Chapter 7

"You won't believe this, Star, but there was a time when I had seriously considered applying to join the Metropolitan Police force," Julia said, as she topped up Star's wine glass.

"Really, what attracted you to it?" Star asked.

"There were lots of reasons, but I suppose having the ability to save an innocent life would be right up there," Julia said, sipping her wine.

"That's a good reason. A police officer will face innumerable situations out on the streets. Some will be simple, and community based, while others can be more complex, but you can be sure that there will almost always be a need to save or protect an innocent person's life. Once an officer has passed their training it becomes their responsibility to act accordingly and protect those innocent members of the public. What I can tell you, Julia, is that the psychological reward when you get home safe and sound knowing that you truly made a difference to someone, somewhere, is off the scale," Star said.

"I can imagine that no two days are the same," Julia said as she slipped off her high heel shoes and sat back in her armchair.

"You would be right. There were times when I'd be travelling to a crime scene somewhere and I'd look out of the window and watch herds of people from every race, colour and creed going to places of work that they probably hated. I would imagine them waking up on a Monday morning and dreading not just what the day holds in store for them, but the whole week. It must be soul destroying knowing you have no choice but to go through the motions, month in month out to just pay their bills and get through another year," Star said as she placed her glass on the coffee table. "The same can very definitely not be said as a police officer. You can believe me when I say that no two days are ever the same. There is always something new and exhilarating. You could be giving directions to a foreign tourist one minute and then be first on the scene of an armed robbery the next. Then of course, with time and training you can move into different departments."

"Like you did?" Julia said with a wry smile.

"Sure, I opted to be more involved with serious crime," said Star.

"I heard that it pays well too," Julia said with a chuckle. "It must do to have a wardrobe like you have."

"It can be, but not always. If a person's primary motivation to join the force is the salary, they would most probably be disappointed. Working your way through a corporation would probably pay significantly more," Star said, running her fingers through her hair.

"It must be nice to give something back too," said Julia.

"I believe that most officers would agree with you. You're not only serving yourself but a broader community. There are very few career choices that could provide the same kind of pride," said Star.

"There must be an awful lot of moral responsibility attached to the job," Julia said as she took another small sip from her wine glass.

"There certainly is," Star said, relaxing her shoulders. "When an officer puts on that uniform or presents their warrant card, their words, actions and behaviour can have a huge influence on members of the public."

"I never really thought about it too deeply but just listening to you, Star, I imagine it's a highly skilled profession," Julia said.

"I'm sure there are people who watch a few television shows and imagine that is the life of a police officer and fail to grasp that to take and pass the entrance exam you require a thorough understanding of logic, maths, reading comprehension, critical thinking skills, high fitness levels and a personal profile that meets the professional needs of a career in the police force," Star explained.

"Wow," Julia said.

"It doesn't end there Julia. Once you've passed your entrance exam and the training at Hendon you'll then, as a qualified police officer, find yourself exposed to further skills," Star said.

"Like what?" Julia said, as she positioned herself to become more comfortable.

"You'll train to become a far more effective driver because you will need those skills to chase down criminals," Star said.

"What else?"

"You'll gain critical thinking skills because, believe me, you will find yourself in highly complex situations. An officer will gain extensive interview skills to isolate the information needed to make their case and be able to see through the lies and deception by reading body language," Star said.

"I was told that we communicate more through body language than we do verbally," Julia said with a slow, seductive, smile.

Star beamed.

"Yes, we do, and yes, you just have," Star said. "So, why didn't you apply?"

"I had a lovely gay friend, Emma; we had known each other since our college days, and she was always going on about how interesting the life of a police officer could be. She did apply and was accepted. I think with her training and with me following my own career path we kind of lost contact, and then one night I saw her out at a gay club in Soho. She said she had become disillusioned, saying that as a new recruit they were treated like children, told what they could and could not do without logical reason. It might have been an isolated incident, but she didn't feel she had the support or back up to effectively do the job that was required to make a difference. Emma told me that eighty percent of the recruits she had trained with had left within two or three years. The impression she got was that the bean counters upstairs were happy to see them leave to save on future pension costs," Julia said.

"I'm sorry to hear that. I can't comment on the current recruitment process although I'd be surprised if what your friend, Emma, said was more her personal perception. Do you know what career path she followed?" Star said before swallowing down the last of her red wine.

"Yes, Emma joined the British Army. We still keep in touch. You know the kind of thing, with an email every so often. She's serving in Afghanistan and has done well with her career. It sounds like she's a lot happier now. Emma was always that front line kind of person," Julia said as she leant forward and reached out for the wine bottle. "Oh, by the way, there was never anything between Emma and me. We were just good friends; besides, she was not my type."

"Really? And what is your type?" Star asked as she placed her hand over her glass.

"Hmm," Julia said as she rubbed her dimpled chin "For a long time I thought that a lesbian was a lesbian. How wrong was I?"

Star left her empty wine glass on the coffee table and sat back on the sofa.

"I can admire the activist for their passion and love of social justice but there is no physical attraction just as there isn't for the butch look. I don't want a woman that looks and acts like a man. The baby dyke straight out of the closet can be a fun, adventurous, liaison. I suppose the kind of woman who really rocks my world is the femme. A beautiful, educated, woman that still identifies as being female and falls neatly into the traditional feminine mannerisms and style. She could easily be mistaken for straight because she wears make-up and every male and female looks at her when she enters the room. Oh, my good lord, I've just described you, Star Bellamy!" Julia exclaimed before rising to her stocking clad feet and slowly walking around to join Star on the sofa."

Star looked up at Julia's pert nose and orchid-pink lips.

"You are stunning." thought Star. *"You could rock my world too."*

"Remind me, have I told you how ravishing you look this evening?" Julia asked as she brushed an imaginary spot of dust from Star's shoulder.

The touch of Julia hand sent shivers of excitement through Star's body.

"You may not have said it out loud, but your body language has had me on the edge of my seat all night," Star said.

"Is that a bad thing?" Julia whispered, as she ran her finger along Star's cheek before taking a strand of hair between her thumb and forefinger and slowly moving it off her face.

Star closed her eyes and slowly exhaled. When she opened her eyes, she was met with Julia's warm smile. Julia slowly leant forward and gave Star a quick peck on her cheek. The eye contact was intense. Star turned to face Julia and slowly they both leant forward until their eyes closed and their lips met. Star could feel Julia's tongue gently enter her mouth. The kiss was sensual, honest and sweet. Julia ran her hand from Star's waist, up the side of her body and then gently cupped her face. Star pulled away momentarily and looked deep into Julia's eyes. Her expression became more intense as she pulled Star forward. Their lips locked and the kissing became increasingly passionate. Julia's breathing became heavier as she kissed Star along her neck and behind her ear. Star found herself gasping as Julia ran her hand over her body. Star pulled away gently.

"Julia, do want to go to your bedroom?" Star whispered with bated breath.

Julia smiled, got to her feet and stretched out her hand. Star took it and the two women locked fingers. Julia led her through to the bedroom.

***

It was 12.30 am when Star's mobile phone rang.

"Who can that be?" Julia said as she looked over towards the open door.

"I have to take that," Star said.

"Really?" Julia said.

"It will be work," Star said as she slid out of the warm bed. She picked her dress up off the floor and slipped it on.

"Sorry Julia," she said as she raced out of the bedroom and into the lounge. She opened her handbag, reached in and grabbed her mobile phone.

"Hello?" she said.

DC Robin Carpenter was on the phone. "Sorry to bother you, Sergeant but there's been an incident outside the Flying Shuttle pub in Tooting."

Star knew the Flying Shuttle pub to be amongst one of the roughest pubs in southwest London. The clientele included drug dealers, armed robbers and working girls. Violence had become so bad that while in uniform, Star had been one of sixteen officers drafted in to close it down in a raid. The pub had turned over several landlords; all of whom had been too scared to call last orders for fear of violence or retribution. The attitude was that the faces that drank there called the shots. Star recalled how, even with sixteen officers, they didn't feel safe. The pub's customers were drunk, aggressive and itching for a fight. The police came away with just a few grams of marijuana. At the council licensing hearing the police were informed that the pub would remain open. Star, like many of the officers, believed that the councillors had either been paid off or had been subject to threats of serious violence.

Star looked down at her watch and shook her head.

"Damn, that's going to take a good half an hour even with the blue strobe on," thought Star.

"Is DI Pratt with you?" Star asked.

"No, Sergeant," DC Robin Carpenter replied. "He said you would handle it."

" Okay, I'm on my way."

"See you shortly." DC Robin Carpenter said.

Star rang off and put the phone back in her handbag.

"Oh shit, what do I do now? What do I say to Julia?" thought Star.

Star paused for several seconds before racing back to the bedroom.

"Julia, I'm so sorry but I have to go," Star said, as she dressed herself quickly.

"Can't someone else cover for you?" Julia pleaded sitting up in bed.

"I've been called in to cover for someone else," Star said, as she slipped her foot into her Christian Louboutin stiletto heels.

"Is that the same person we touched on at the restaurant the other night?" Julia asked.

Star nodded.

"So shit rolls downhill no matter what profession you're in," Julia hissed.

"I'm sorry Julia, it's all part of the job," Star said before leaning over the bed and kissing Julia on the lips. "Believe me I would rather be in there with you."

"I would rather you be in here too," Julia said, sulking.

"I'll call you tomorrow," Star called out as she bolted out of the bedroom, down the hallway and out the front door.

She got into her Range Rover, secured the seat belt, and started the engine. Star rarely drank more than a glass or two of red wine and if the temptation to drink more was there, she left her car and took a taxicab home. This evening Star had only consumed one and a half glasses which equated to approximately 24mgs of alcohol. The legal limit was 80mg per 100ml of blood or 35 micrograms of breath although Star understood that there were no hard and fast rules as to how much you could legally drink without falling foul of the law. The rate at which the body absorbs the alcohol depends on a series of factors that includes gender, weight and stress levels.

Star sped across London with the blue strobe light flashing through the grill and flashing her main beam lights. The roads were reasonably clear with little traffic. Star slowed down at the traffic lights to avoid an accident but continued to maintain her speed until she arrived outside the Flying Shuttle pub in Tooting. She climbed out of her car, closed and locked the door. Robin was talking to a uniformed officer and stopped when he saw Star.

"Sergeant," DC Robin Carpenter called.

Star looked around the crime scene. There several people on the opposite side looking on.

"Where are we?" Star asked as she continued to scan the area.

"The uniforms were first on the scene. That's him, over there, PC Craig Marvin," DC Robin Carpenter said.

Star looked up and waved the police constable over.

"I'm Detective Sergeant Star Bellamy. My Detective Constable tells me you were the first on the scene," said Star.

"Yes Sergeant. I did an initial assessment of the situation. I saw that a man was injured, possibly by gun shots. I checked for a pulse and discovered there wasn't one, so I called for an ambulance and back up. Individuals from the pub began to wander off. I tried to keep as many people as I could behind so I could take a witness statement, but they all claimed to have seen nothing. However, one gentleman was out walking his dog when he claimed that a black BMW had been parked outside the pub with two large men in it. The gentleman thought that they looked suspicious and made a mental note of the vehicle registration number."

"Excellent," Star said.

"He said that a man left the pub, which he thought was strange because of the time, when a large, heavily built man got out of the car. I asked for a description which he gave as a white male, possibly mid-forties, nineteen, maybe twenty stone and a good six foot three tall. The two men talked for a few seconds. There was a loud exchange of words. It was then that the man that had left the pub produced a large knife. The larger man shoved him, pulled out a gun and shot him three times before getting back into the car and racing away." PC Craig Marvin said before closing his note pad.

"Did the witness say what the exchange of words was about?" Star asked as she looked over the constable's shoulder where she noticed the crime scene had been preserved with a tape barrier.

"He said it sounded like 'Get in the motor you slag!'"

"Okay, that's all for now. Thank you," Star said.

"Robin, what do we know about the victim?" Star asked as she watched officers recover bullet shells from the ground, then label and package them into sealed polythene bags.

"Sergeant, we believe the victim to be Thomas Deane," DC Robin Carpenter said in a lowered tone. "He was a registered police informer. Local officers have been using him to gather intelligence on the pub's customers. Pretty serious lot by all accounts Sergeant. Maybe he slipped up?" DC Robin Carpenter said.

"What do know about the registration number the dog walker took?" Star said as she scanned the area for the dog walker.

"The number plate is registered to a car that was involved in a motor vehicle accident three years ago, written off by the insurance company, and then crushed," DC Robin Carpenter replied.

"Was the written off car also a BMW?" Star asked.

"Yes, Sergeant, it matched the car's description."

"We're dealing with professional criminals here. We need to know what information Thomas Deane was passing back and about who," Star said.

"I'm on it, Sergeant," DC Robin Carpenter replied.

Chapter 8

"Move, you slags!" Buster growled as he shoved one of the hooded criminals that had lagged behind the eleven petty villains, grasses and known police informers he'd had rounded up from all over London and shoved, tied and bound, into the back of a small truck.

Buster nodded to his four armed associates. They turned each of the hooded kidnapped men to face the same direction. There were tears, whimpers and pleas of innocence but it all fell on deaf ears.

"Take the hoods off," Buster commanded.

Buster Cummings was an old school London face with a fearsome reputation as an unlicensed boxer, enforcer and bodyguard. Weighing in at just over nineteen stone, he was six foot five and with over one thousand unlicensed fights to his credit, he was considered by those in the underworld to be the unofficial heavy weight champion of Great Britain. As a teenager he had mixed with criminals from all over London; emulating the stories they had heard about the Richardson's from South London, the Kray Twins, and The Nash family from North London. The lads would regularly meet up at a local pub in Bermondsey to share stories of their week's takings when a local bully boy and self-appointed bouncer decided he wanted to remove the motley crew from the pub. Buster took umbrage at the thirty-year-old's mouthing off, disrespecting him and trying to throw his weight around. He was up, on his feet and threw a right hook with such ferocity that it sent the local hard man sprawling across the beer-stained carpet. Buster stood over the unconscious body with both fists tightly clenched and ready to finish the job. That was a turning point for Buster; realising he could make a good living with his fists. In the criminal underworld Buster Cummings was both feared and respected. He ran security for the Fenton Family.

The Fenton Family - also known as the Fenton Firm - was a criminal organisation that was believed by many of those in the underworld and the authorities to be one of the most powerful criminal organisations in the United Kingdom, with an alleged wealth of over three hundred million pounds. Their activities included loan sharking, armed robbery, racketeering, drug trafficking, murder, human trafficking, extortion, bribery, pimping, money laundering, fraud, arms trafficking and contract killing. Shirley Fenton became the head of the organisation after her husband, Terry, was brutally murdered during a drug related gangland conflict. The rival gang underestimated the drive, determination and the violence that the pretty blonde was capable of. Every member of the rival gang was tracked down and murdered, many by Shirley's own hands. The leader, fearing for his life, bought a counterfeit passport and fled to Tenerife in the Canary Islands. Within a month he had been found and was mowed down outside a nightclub by a machine gun from a passing motorcycle. Shirley Fenton had cemented her position as matriarch of the Fenton Firm and brought her sons, Connor, Reece and Brandon into the front line of the family business.

From out of the shadows a slim, shapely, figure emerged.

"Please, I don't know what I've supposed to have done," one of the men called out.

"Whatever it is I know it wasn't me," another called out as his hood was removed.

"Oh fuck, its Shirley Fenton," sighed one of the kidnapped men, as he lowered his head.

Shirley Fenton stood a little over five foot seven tall. She had a svelte, hourglass figure which was accentuated by the dark blue pinstripe skirt, matching jacket and stiletto heels that she wore. Locks of Shirley's moon gleam gold hair curtained over her heart shaped face.

"Gentlemen, thank for meeting with me. My apologies if some of the firm were a little heavy handed," Shirley said with a broad smile.

"Who the fuck do you fucking Fenton's think you are!" one of the men yelled.

Shirley reached into her handbag and produced a Beretta 92FS 9mm semi-automatic handgun and fired.

BANG! BANG! BANG!

"Oh, I'm sorry, were you addressing me?" Shirley said calmly as the man fell to the ground.

BANG! BANG! BANG!

"What's that, the cat got your tongue?" Shirley said as she moved several steps closer to her target

BANG! BANG! BANG!

"Have you finished?" Shirley said as she lowered the gun to her side.

The remaining tied men were jostling from left to right as the sounds of the gunshots ricochet around the empty, disused, abattoir. One elderly villain stood motionless as urine ran down his legs, through the bottom of his trousers and onto the concrete floor.

"I have had Buster bring you here because I have a problem, and you gentlemen may be in a position to help me. My son, Brandon, went missing two days ago. He failed to attend an important family business meeting which is something that he would never do. The police, who are on our payroll, have very kindly tracked his car to Clapham Junction, but there's no sign of him. He's not answering his phone which, as you can see, is causing me some concern. What is the word out on the streets, who is taking a shot at the title and where is my son?" Shirley asked as she stood over the dead body.

There was silence as each of the men looked at each other, clearly bewildered.

BANG! BANG! BANG!

Shirley fired three more shots into the bullet riddled body.

"Please Mrs Fenton, I don't know anything. There is no one out there brave or stupid enough to take a pop at the Fenton's," one of the men said.

"Maybe it's the Russians," offered one of the men as a solution.

"Or the Albanians," said another.

Shirley shook her head slowly.

"I don't need maybes or what ifs. What I do need to know is who is behind the liberty and where my son is being held."

The men were all shaking heads and shrugging their shoulders.

"Do you need a little more motivation to loosen your tongues?" Shirley said as she nodded at Buster.

Immediately each member of the firm raised their handguns and took aim.

"Mrs Fenton, please, can't you see that we don't know anything. If we did, we would have spilt the beans long before you took the first shot," reasoned one of the men.

"What's his name, Buster?" Shirley said as she lowered the gun.

"Jack Williams from Hackbridge, Mrs Fenton. He drinks in The Skinners Arms," Buster said.

"Okay, Jack Williams from Hackbridge, I want you to start calling in favours, knock on some doors and find out whatever you can and then you pass that information back to Buster," Shirley said as she put the gun back in her handbag. "Can you do that for me?"

Jack began nodding his head emphatically.

"Buster, put a few quid expenses in each of their pockets and send them on their way. Oh, and get rid of that disrespectful piece of shit," Shirley said, pointing at the bloody corpse.

Buster nodded and motioned his boys to start putting the hoods back on the heads of the remaining kidnapped men before herding them back into the back of the truck that had brought them to the former abattoir.

"What's the next move, Mum?" Conner, the youngest son, asked.

Connor was a university graduate from Roehampton with a BSc in Business and Financial Management. From an early age he had demonstrated an avid interest in numbers. Connor Fenton headed the team that managed their legitimate business interests and laundered the money from criminal enterprises.

"I'm not sure," Shirley muttered, slowly shaking her head.

"What about leveraging some of the old bill we have on the payroll?" Reece said.

Reece Fenton had gained an early reputation in London's underworld as a brutal, cold-blooded murderer and was suspected by the police to have been directly involved in thirty-six crime related deaths over a four year period. While Connor had been studying at University, Reece had been charged with armed robbery. However, despite compelling evidence being submitted by the crown prosecution, the key police evidence to substantiate the prosecutions claims had been lost. Reece was found not guilty and took a key role in the family's criminal affairs, answering only to his older brother Brandon and the family's matriarch, Shirley.

"Let's make the call," Shirley said. "I want your brother Brandon back. Whatever it takes."

"Leave it to me, mum," Reece replied.

Chapter 9

Despite the late night, Star was back in her office before 8.00 am. She had made herself a cup of coffee and sat behind her desk thinking about Julia and the previous evening. Star reached for her mobile phone and sent a text message.

'Good morning, Julia, I hope you slept well.'

Star re-read the text message and shook her head.

"You've got to do better than that," thought Star as she tapped out a second text message.

'I'm sorry I had to leave so quickly.'

Star read the text message over and again shook her head.

"That is simply not enough Star! Just go ahead and tell her how you really feel," Star thought as she typed out a third text message.

'Hi Julia, behind my casual messages are a myriad of emotions that are just too complex to comprehend. Thank you for a wonderful evening. Can you forgive my rapid departure? xxx'

"Well if that doesn't do it, I don't know what will," thought Star.

A loud knock on her office door brought her back to work mode.

"Come in," Star called out.

The door opened.

"Good morning DS Bellamy."

"Hello Deepika. I haven't seen you in ages. How are you?"

"Can we talk?" Detective Constable Deepika Kumar said as she closed the office door.

"Of course, take a seat," Star said. "How can I help you?"

"I have tried, and I mean tried desperately to fit in and become the kind of police officer that would make me feel proud when I look in the mirror, but for every two steps forward I take, the homophobic, racist and discriminating behaviours by my fellow police officers, including those of senior rank push back, and it is no longer tolerable," DC Deepika Kumar said with a deep sigh. "I can only describe my feelings as depression, oppression and repression. My heart skips a beat when the phone on my desk rings. My fear is that it'll be another nuisance call with someone telling yet another racist joke. If they wanted me to feel intimidated, they have succeeded."

"Can I ask for a name?" Star said.

"Detective Sergeant Bellamy this is more than just one bad apple. The whole bloody barrel is rotten, and it doesn't matter how many good apples you put in it! At first I let the occasional Paki remark or dirty look slide by, but it just got worse. The final nail in the coffin was when a senior officer, who I will not name just yet, told another officer to fetch me once I'd finished working in the corner shop."

"I'm really sorry to hear this," Star said.

"Three months ago, I decided to keep a log of what can only be described as racist behaviour. I now have a timed and dated log with what was said by whom, the comments that followed and the names of those that witnessed it. I have found this whole disgusting episode intense and deeply stressful and right now I'm seriously considering what my next move is," DC Deepika Kumar said.

"What do you want me to do? How can I help?" Star said.

DC Deepika Kumar paused for a few moments.

"I would like you to share this conversation with Detective Inspector Ronald Pratt who may or may not be featured in my log."

"I can do that," Star said.

"Thank you, Star, you're one of the good apples," DC Deepika Kumar said as she stood to leave.

"I'll come back to you," said Star.

DC Deepika Kumar smiled, nodded, and left the office. Star looked down at her watch. She grabbed her file and made her way to DI Pratt's office. She knocked on his closed door.

"Yes!"

"Detective Sergeant Bellamy, sir," Star said, rolling her eyes.

"Come in, come in!"

Star opened the door and found DI Pratt sitting behind his desk. He had just placed the last of the paperwork sprawled out on his desk into a black suitcase. Star spotted a pair of white gloves on the corner of the desk. When he spotted her gaze, he quickly reached out and put them in his open drawer.

"Take a seat, Sergeant."

"Thank you, sir," Star said as she pulled the chair away from the desk.

"Right, where are we with last night's murder at the Flying Shuttle in Tooting?"

Star took the Inspector through everything she had gained from her time at the crime scene. Without looking up, DI Pratt scrawled down some notes.

"I know what you're doing," Star thought. *"You'll be off upstairs making out that you were the first senior officer at the crime scene."*

"Do you have any thoughts about who or why?" DI Pratt said as he finally looked up at Star.

"This is more than a drunken pub fight that got out of hand. I don't why or who is responsible, yet, only that the victim, Thomas Deane, was a police informer. We're making enquiries into what intelligence was being gathered and about whom," Star said as she leant back in her chair.

"Good, keep me in the loop on any developments," DI Pratt said. "Okay, is that it?"

"Actually, sir I need talk to you about a rather delicate matter," Star said.

"Oh no, not another unplanned pregnancy, is it? Who will we lose this time?" DI Pratt said as he leaned back in his chair and crossed both arms.

Star was shocked by the sexist remark.

"No sir, that isn't it."

Star went on to explain the conversation she had had with DC Deepika Kumar.

"Does she know who wears the pants around here?" DI Pratt said with a scowl.

"She does, sir, which is why she asked me to speak to you," Star said.

"It all sounds like a bit of harmless banter. She should suck it up and just get on with the job!" DI Pratt said, as he slapped the corner of the desk with his open palm.

"Sir, Detective Constable Deepika Kumar has kept a log with names, dates and witnesses and is now considering her options," Star said.

Star saw the look of horror on DI Pratt's face.

"Who has she named?"

"She didn't say sir. Only that it included senior officers," Star said.

"We don't need another mess dragged through the press," DI Pratt said shaking his head.

"More importantly, sir, these issues matter to the individuals. These behaviours are out-dated at best and harmful at worst. Unless we as a force tackle everyday racism, homophobia and sexism in the workplace then the most innovative policies and initiatives designed to advance equality will fail and the police force will be unable to deliver the changes needed," Star said.

"That's a very good point, Sergeant, and my thoughts exactly. I want you to meet with Detective Constable Kumar and find out exactly what it is that she wants," DI Pratt said.

"Are you asking me to negotiate a compromise agreement, sir?"

"Use your initiative to resolve the issue, Sergeant," DI Pratt said as he rubbed his chin.

"I will, sir," said Star.

"Oh, I've had a message from upstairs. We have a missing person's report that I want you to personally handle."

"Missing persons, sir? That's not what we do," Star said abruptly.

DI Pratt reached into his jacket pocket. He took out a post-it note and handed it to Star.

"You're to meet Mrs Shirley Fenton at 3.00 pm this afternoon at her home address. Keep me in the loop."

Star looked down at the note.

"Shirley Fenton, the Fenton Firm. This is major league," thought Star.

"You do know who the Fentons are?" DI Pratt said sharply.

"Yes sir. I've heard them referred to as the Teflon Mob because we have failed to make anything stick. My understanding was that both MI5 and the Inland Revenue combined forces and set up a secret squad to dismantle the Fenton's international crime organisation but failed when the head of the organisation, Terry Fenton, was murdered. They are serious, extremely serious, people. I don't understand why they would call us in," Star said with a quizzical expression.

"Just make the call and keep me informed," DI Pratt said without looking up from his desk.

"Yes sir."

Star got up, slid the chair back behind the desk and left the Inspector's office. She felt excited and strangely exhilarated that she would get to meet *the* Shirley Fenton - head of the most powerful crime organisation in the United Kingdom.

"Sergeant,"

Star turned around to see DC Robin Carpenter walking towards her.

"Yes, Robin," Star said.

"Thomas Deane has been feeding back information about all and sundry in Tooting. There isn't anything major league, but the information he's been passing back has sent down scores of street level villains. The queue of people with a motive, if his cover was blown, would be as long as your arm," DC Robin Carpenter said. "This may be nothing, but I did come across a couple of reports of people being bundled into cars."

"Follow it up, please Robin. We need to follow any leads we can before the case goes cold," Star said.

"Yes, Sergeant."

Star's mobile phone pinged. It was a text message.

'Good morning, Star. You're forgiven. Wish you were here right now……. xxx'

Star beamed and put the phone back into her handbag.

Chapter 10

Star left her office in good time for her meeting with Shirley Fenton. She took a slow drive across London to Kensington. She drove by her home and then past Kensington Palace Gardens. Her thoughts were suddenly taken back to her childhood. Star's mother, Jennifer, would take her into the grounds of Kensington Palace gardens. Her memories were always of beautiful sunny days that seemed to last forever. Jennifer and Star would stroll through 'Cradle Walk', an arched arbour of red-twigged lime. The shady tunnel provided shade for mother and daughter to look out in awe at the bright colours in the sunken gardens. Star would watch the aged gardener pruning the foliage in order to promote new growth. Jennifer would tell stories about the family's long history in Kensington and how her great, great grandmother was first gifted with the power to communicate with the dead.

Star entered the prestigious Cheyne Walk in Chelsea SW3 and parked behind a blue Bentley Mulsanne. The private registration number plate read 'S1 FEN'. Star looked up in awe at the iconic, grade II listed home that overlooked the river Thames.

"This home has got to be worth thirty million pounds if not more," Star thought.

A smartly dressed chauffeur got out of the driver's side door and began to wipe the windscreen with a cloth. Just as Star was going to get out of the car her mobile phone rang.

"Hello?"

"Sergeant, I've followed up on those leads and it appears that the man responsible for the potential abductions fits the same description as the one at the Tooting crime scene," DC Robin Carpenter said.

"Good work Robin. Keep at it."

"Thank you, Sergeant. Just one more thing. They all described the same BMW. I'll get back to work and keep you informed." DC Robin Carpenter said.

"Thank you."

Star put her mobile phone onto silent and walked towards the period townhouse. The chauffeur smiled and tipped his cap. Star returned the smile before stopping by the gloss black six panel hardwood front door. Before she could press the doorbell, the door opened.

"Good afternoon. I'm Detective Sergeant Star Bellamy. I believe Mrs Fenton is expecting me," Star said as she looked up at the huge monster of a man dressed in a tailor fitted black pin-stripe suit, white shirt and black tie.

"You're expected Detective Sergeant," Buster Cummings said as he opened the door and welcomed her in.

Buster led her through the hallway. They entered a room lined with bookshelves. By the open fireplace were two Regency-style leather padded armchairs and a hardwood coffee table.

The door opened and Shirley Fenton entered the room.

"Detective Sergeant Star Bellamy, thank you for coming," Shirley Fenton said as she motioned for Star to take a seat. "Buster, could you organise some coffee please?"

Star couldn't help feeling the overwhelming presence Shirley carried as she entered the room. She projected an immediate sense of ease, poise and self-assurance. She wore a royal blue slim fit blazer with gold buttons and a matching knee length skirt with black nylons and black leather Christian Louboutin Pigalle Follie pointed toe heels.

Buster nodded and left the room, closing the door firmly behind him.

"You appear to be well thought of by your superiors and from what I've learned you're an accomplished police officer in your own right. Sadly, the same cannot be said for your inspector, but then, like all dinosaurs, they become extinct with time," Shirley said as she leant back in her chair.

"I suppose the same could be said of those on the opposite side of the fence," Star said as she met Shirley's gaze head on.

"That might be just a little naive," Shirley said as she shook her head. "If you remove the head of a snake then another grows back to fill the void. That is just the simple supply and demand law of economics."

"Maybe it's just a question of one's moral compass," said Star.

"Shit, why did I say that? Stop being so damn confrontational, you're here to do a job" thought Star.

Shirley paused for a moment and smiled.

"Moral compass, interesting. You mean like that of the establishment who created the police force in order to protect the rich and impose their will? Therefore they control the working classes. The very same establishment that sent almost nine hundred thousand men to their deaths and another one and a half million that were seriously wounded because... Archduke Franz Ferdinand was assassinated. Maybe we should fast forward this moral compass of the ruling elite to a British Prime Minister, a self-appointed spokesperson of the working classes who deliberately blurred the lines between what he knew and what he believed with unjustified certainly that Saddam Hussein was in possession of weapons of mass destruction. The end result was over two hundred thousand men, woman and children lost their lives in a violent, bloody conflict. One cannot help but wonder if the conflict was truly about weapons of mass destruction, regime change or, and here's some food for thought, Detective Sergeant, maybe the objective was to gain direct access to the world's fifth largest oil reserves," Shirley Fenton said as she placed a folded piece of writing paper on the table.

The door opened and a housemaid entered carrying a silver coffee service. She placed it on the coffee table and left the room.

"She's certainly courageous, stands up for what she believes and refuses to stay silent with her opinions when faced with the abuse of power. Her combination of power, self-respect and timing is impressive. I can imagine her being a worthy adversary to the most diligent of police officers or the most blood thirsty, power hungry, criminals," Star thought.

"Do you like coffee, Sergeant?" Shirley Fenton said as she began to pour the black liquid into the cups.

"Yes, I do, thank you, and please forgive me, I didn't mean to appear to be confrontational," Star said as she leant forward to inhale the coffee fumes.

"Hmm, that does smell good," she said.

"The establishment creates the rules for the general population to live by. Some choose to live outside their rules and are not afraid to clash if necessary, so the two parties choose to co-exist. A compromise if you will, but we can debate the broader moral compass subject another time," Shirley said with a wry smile.

Star raised her cup and tasted the coffee.

"This is delicious. I don't think I've ever tasted anything quite like it," she said.

"Coffee, the Black Ivory variety, is one of my few weaknesses. I was introduced to it while travelling in Northern Thailand on business. Would you like to know the process?"

Star nodded as she took a second sip.

"Arabica cherries are fed to the elephants on their plantations. The berries are broken down and digested by the elephants. The farmers then collect the beans from their faeces. That slight bitter taste you're experiencing is where the elephant's enzymes break down the unwanted proteins. Personally, I find it smooth, unique and a great tasting cup of coffee," Shirley Fenton said as she placed the empty cup on the table. "Now, can we please move onto the business of my missing son, Brandon?"

Star was a little taken back by Shirley's ability to completely compartmentalise conversations.

"Yes, of course," Star said as she savoured the last drop of coffee.

"My son has been kidnapped," Shirley said firmly.

"Are you sure? Could he have met someone and just gone rogue for a few days?" Star asked as she produced a note pad from her pocket.

"I'm sure," Shirley said as she slid the folded note paper over the table towards Star.

Star reached out and opened the handwritten note.

> Mrs Fenton we have your son Brandon.
> If you want to see him alive again you
> must follow our instructions. You will be
> Contacted with instructions to bring
> £500,000 in cash. Do not contact the
> Police or Brandon will die!

"When did you receive this?" Star asked as she took a photo of the ransom note with her phone.

"I had a phone call late yesterday from Brandon's phone. The man's voice was muffled but he gave me instructions to pick up an envelope from a telephone box in Cockspur Street, Trafalgar Square. I had it collected and brought it back here. I told him we didn't have half a million pounds in cash just lying around the house and needed some time. We're now waiting for a second phone call to make the drop," Shirley said, her voice choking slightly.

"Do you have any suspicions about who this could be?" Star asked as she readied her pen to start making notes.

"You would need a much bigger note pad than that, Detective Sergeant, to list our enemies. From what we've been able to glean, this is not one of the usual suspects. Everything about the kidnapping is amateurish at best which means we cannot leverage our connections and that is why my son, Reece, insisted we reach out to the authorities to approach the problem from a different angle. I do not care about the money, but what I do want is my eldest son, Brandon, back at home with his family. Everything else is arbitrary," Shirley Fenton said as she poured a second cup of coffee.

"I'll need to take the ransom note for forensics. We have access to a team of handwriting experts, and I'd like them to look at this as well," Star said.

"That's fine. I'm the only person that has handled it," Shirley said. "Here is a recent picture of Brandon."

"Did the kidnapper indicate when he would be calling again to get the ransom?" Star said as she slid the ransom note and photograph inside her folder.

"I told him we needed a couple of days to generate that kind of cash. So he should call tomorrow."

"Okay, I'll have a sports holdall bag fitted out with a GPS so we can track the money and the kidnappers, and find your son," said Star.

As Shirley put her empty coffee cup on the table, the door opened, Buster entered the room and pointed to his watch.

"Okay, Buster give me five minutes," Shirley said.

"Buster, is it?" Star asked as she rose to her feet.

Buster nodded.

"Can I ask where you were at 12.30 am two nights ago?" said Star.

Buster didn't answer.

"Why would you ask that?" Shirley said as she stood up.

"There was an incident in Tooting and Buster fits the witness description," said Star.

"Buster was here with me, my two sons, Connor and Reece, two of the family barristers and a prominent member of parliament. All of which would happily provide you with statements to that effect if required, Sergeant," Shirley said abruptly.

"I'm sure that will not be necessary," Star said. "I'll be back tomorrow morning."

"Once again, thank you Detective Sergeant Bellamy," Shirley said nodding.

Buster led Star back out into the hallway. Immediately Star could feel it was ice cold. Her eyes were drawn to the staircase where she spotted a tall figure at the top of the stairs. Initially she could not distinguish the image as being a man or woman. It had all the strong features of a man despite the heavy face foundation, thick eye liner and ruby red lipstick. The brown hair that toppled over her shoulders had the appearance of a wig. The apparition wore a black cardigan and skirt with a white and red striped blouse, white nylons and black patent high heels. It stared down at Star for several seconds before fading away.

Star had just seen the apparition of a cross-dresser. A term used for gay men and woman who dress in clothes of the opposite sex.

"Did you just see that?" Star said, pointing towards the top of the stairs.

"See what?" replied Buster as he opened the front door.

"Oh, nothing," Star said, "I thought I saw a black cat."

"We don't have any animals in the house," Buster grunted.

The door was closed firmly. Star took several steps and then looked back at the house. She thought she caught a glimpse of Shirley by the second-floor window. Star passed the chauffeur who was still cleaning the headlamps. He looked up and gave her an awkward smile. She took her keys from her handbag and pressed the central locking button. When she opened the car door, she saw a note on the passenger side car seat. She immediately looked up and over at the chauffeur who was still wiping the same head lamp. Star started the car and drove out of Cheyne Walk. Once she was out of sight she pulled over and read the note.

Brandon was not all he appeared to his family. They are looking in all the wrong places. Visit the Rainbow Club.

"This must have been from the chauffeur," thought Star.

Star turned the car around, crossed the Albert Bridge and then followed the Chelsea embankment. She arrived at the Rainbow Club in Soho within a few minutes. Star parked directly outside the club which was tucked between an Italian restaurant and a sex shop. She waved her warrant card at the traffic warden who was strutting furiously towards her. Star walked cautiously down the three steps to the club door. It was open so she entered.

"Hello sweetheart, are you a member?"

Star looked at the elderly man standing by the reception dressed in a purple ankle length dress as he drew heavily on his cigarette.

"No," replied Star as she showed him her warrant card, "I'm following up on a lead."

"If you're not a member, sweetie, then you can't come in here, sorry," said the man as he shrugged his shoulders.

"I just need a few minutes to look around," Star said. "Please."

"No can do. Not even for a pretty please. Rules are rules. It's strictly a members-only club."

"I was really hoping to avoid getting a search warrant and coming back at what, midnight?" Star said as she looked for a crack in his blunt demeanour.

"Search warrant!"

"Like I said, I only need a few minutes to look around," said Star.

Star watched as the receptionist stubbed out his cigarette and then fiddled awkwardly with his fingers.

"Just a few minutes, you say?"

Star smiled and gave a quick nod.

"Okay but if anybody asks why you're here it's because you're thinking about taking a membership, okay?"

Star beamed and followed the receptionist through a double set of doors.

"We cater for all tastes and fetishes here. Over there," said the receptionist, "is an adult cinema where couples or singles are invited to take a seat and watch adult films. Over here is the bar and behind that there are several rooms with split doors where members can engage in their fantasies. The top half of the door can remain open if groups are open to spectators. We call that the dogging experience or they can be closed and locked for those who something a little more private. Every room is geared towards a particular fetish that includes a classroom, complete with a blackboard, chalk and rubbers if you'll excuse the pun. We have dungeons with torture equipment and a room that houses a large tent for those who enjoy watching the silhouettes at play. What we have to offer our select members is a safe and friendly environment where they leave their dull, vanilla, lives outside and just come and do their own thing. Once again, you'll have to excuse the pun," the receptionist chortled as he placed both hands on his hips.

Star spotted a wall with several framed photographs.

"Were you considering something for the policeman's ball? We really do cater for all sorts here!" said the receptionist with a sarcastic twang.

Star tipped her head to one side and scowled.

"Sorry," said the receptionist, shaking her head and looking visibly uncomfortable.

One of the photographs on the wall looked exactly like the cross-dressing apparition she had seen in Cheyne walk.

"Who is this?" Star said as she pointed directly to the image on the photograph.

"Oh, that's Lady Devine. She is extremely popular here, a proper little live wire," said the receptionist.

Star took out her mobile phone and took a photograph.

"You can't do that!" the receptionist said adamantly.

"I'm a big fan. I'm sure Lady Devine won't mind," Star said as she turned on her heels and began to strut back towards the entrance. "Thank you for your time, you've been very helpful."

"Well, I never," growled the receptionist as he struggled to keep pace.

Star scampered up the steps of the club and climbed back into the Range Rover. She reached over for the ransom note and the picture of Brandon Fenton. She looked down at her phone and the photo. Lady Devine was the apparition she had seen at Cheyne walk and Brandon Fenton was Lady Devine. The kidnapping had become a murder case.

Chapter 11

"I've spoken at length with Detective Inspector Pratt, Deepika and he's asked to me to find a compromise. A place where both parties can move on amicably," said Star.

"If I were her, I'd drag this through the courts so that every last one of them lost their jobs and exposed them for the nasty, horrible, racist bullies that they are," thought Star.

"I don't want this to get any worse than it already is," Detective Constable Deepika Kumar said as she handed Star an estate agent's vending sheet. "This is what it will take to make me and my little black book simply go away. My solicitor has been made aware of the situation and is in possession of the book. He has been instructed to make its contents public should I suddenly fall ill, get knocked down by a hit and run driver or get shot in a failed robbery attempt."

"There's no need for that," Star said as she read through the vending sheet. "Nobody here would hurt you."

Deepika shook her head slowly.

"Not that long ago a major newspaper published a dossier which revealed how the police routinely and deliberately concealed vital evidence in order to frustrate a defendant's case. It disclosed the tactics and deep-seated cultural practices that actively encouraged officers to hide and withhold vital information which could undermine the Crown Prosecution Service. Not only were police officers tampering with evidence which could result in an innocent party being incarcerated, but training was also being given to show officers how to avoid making material available which might undermine their cases. Can you imagine that, Star, police officers being trained to withhold evidence? I was and am still stunned by that. It's almost as if fabricating evidence, lying or tampering with evidence is seen, by some officers, as fair game. So, would I feel at risk from senior officers by coming forward and putting their pensions on the line? Yes. Would I put it past a senior officer to suggest to a criminal afraid of a custodial sentence that all the evidence could disappear if something were to happen to me? I am sad to say, Star, that yes, I believe that could happen, so I've taken the appropriate actions to protect myself," Deepika said as she crossed her arms.

"I can't comment Detective Constable Kumar," said Star.

"See that?" said Deepika. "One minute we're Deepika and Star and the next we're calling each other by our ranks."

"What exactly are you asking me for?" Star asked, ignoring the comment.

"I want that house as the compromise agreement and I want the answer by Monday, latest, as the agent is holding the house for me. Failure to agree will result in, well, you know what. You're a good police officer Detective Sergeant Bellamy and represent all that is essential, in my view, in a modern, progressive, police force and I'm sorry that I have had to involve you," said Deepika.

"Should your request be accepted, you will be expected to sign a non-disclosure agreement. Will that be an issue?"

"If they buy me that house I'll disappear into the sunset and forget about ever being in the police force. Does that answer your question?"

"Thank you for bringing this issue to my attention. I will report back and do all that I can to bring this upsetting business to an amicable conclusion," said Star.

"By Monday latest," Deepika said firmly.

"I'll do my personal best," said Star.

"That's more than enough for me, Star. Like I said, you are one of the good apples," Deepika said as she rose to her feet. "With your agreement I'm going to clear my desk of personal affects and then quietly leave the building without speaking to anyone. You have my mobile telephone number on record. All I need now is to know if we've reached a compromise or not."

"I'll call you," said Star.

Deepika silently mouthed 'I'm sorry' and left Star's office.

Star rubbed her head several times and then opted to go down to the canteen for a coffee before reporting her meeting with Shirley Fenton and the outcome with Deepika. She had stayed late the previous night, having had the forensic team examine the handwritten ransom note and place a GPS tracking device inside a branded sports holdall. Julia had messaged, inviting her for dinner which Star had to decline. A second message was sent at 11.00 pm inviting Star to join her for a nightcap. Star had worked a solid fifteen hours and was struggling to keep her eyes open. As much as she wanted to join Julia, she needed to sleep and so declined her kind offer for the second time.

Initially Star had fallen into a deep sleep but gently fell into a dream:

Star left the police station on foot. To her left and right were all the people and their friends she had arrested, interviewed and convicted during her career. Behind her were the police officers she knew to be part of all that was wrong. Their faces were contorted and filled with hate. Star was in danger. Together, all those to her left and right produced machete's, knives, clubs and axes. Behind her the police held tasers, stun guns and truncheons. Detective Inspector Pratt pushed his way through the officers. He held an MP5 sub-machine gun. He yelled out at the top of his voice, 'Kill her!" and then fired the semi-automatic weapon into the air. Star saw an opening ahead of her. She kicked off her heels and bolted away. With the sound of gunshots behind her she ran through the empty streets. She glanced over her shoulder to see the streets packed with an angry mob of crazed people hungry for her blood. Star ran through a junction; cars came to a screeching halt, narrowly missing her. The screaming mob were close as she approached her home. Outside her apartment block was a blue Bentley Mulsanne. Star was gasping for air as she forced her legs to keep up the pace. The door of the Bentley opened. Star could see a stocking clad leg and then Shirley Fenton stepped out the car. She carried an M16 assault rifle.

"Star, get behind me!" she called out.

As Star stepped behind Shirley Fenton, she opened fire. Exhausted, Star's legs had given way and she found herself crouching down on the pavement. Shirley Fenton mowed down line after line of criminals, crooks, villains and dubious police officers. Their bodies fell into heaps across the road. Shirley reloaded and kept firing until every last one of Star's pursuers were either mortally wounded or dead. Detective Inspector Pratt rose from behind a mound of dead bodies. Before he could open fire, Shirley rapidly took a single head shot. DI Pratt dropped his weapon and looked skyward before falling dead to the ground. Shirley threw her weapon onto the back seat of her car and then turned to face Star with her hand outstretched. Star looked up to see the dark grey skies clearing. The sun began to shine as she took Shirley's hand and was helped gently to her feet. Star found herself gazing into Shirley's eyes. Star was now on her feet, but her hand was still firmly in Shirley's. The two women hadn't broken eye contact. Star could feel a strong sexual attraction, her heart beat faster and she longed to be held in her arms. Shirley slowly edged forward and whispered 'we were meant to be lovers', as her hand slid down her back to the base of her spine. Her hand tensed and brought her closer. With Shirley just millimetres away from her lips, the alarm on her mobile phone went off and she woke up.

Star pondered over the meaning of the dream while in the shower, over breakfast and in the car on her way to the office. She was still thinking about it when Peter Eldridge first entered her office.

"Star, is that you?"

Star looked up to see her friend Peter Eldridge from the SC019 (Specialist Crime & Operations) Armed Response Unit. The two had become friends while undergoing their Jiu Jitsu training and regularly sparred together. Peter, with his military background, went on to train in specialist unarmed close quarter combat, advanced firearms and tactical pursuit driving.

"Hello Peter, wow, it must be what, six months?" Star said as she put her change into the vending machine.

"More like a year, Star."

Star looked him up and down. He wore black overalls made from flame retardant material, boots and was carrying his gloves.

"I see you're still with the Armed Response Unit," Star said with a chuckle. "Either that or you're on your way to a fancy-dress party."

"Oh, how very droll, Star Bellamy. I'll have you know that I was seconded to the Trojan Proactive Unit. Unlike the ARV who patrol or wait on standby until they're needed, we're responsible for patrolling high risk areas," Peter said as he took his coffee from the machine.

Star and Peter sat in the canteen.

"How has life been treating you?" Peter said before blowing the top of his hot coffee.

"Some good, some bad, but mostly good," said Star. "What about you?"

"Well, the missus finally left me. She blamed the job, but I think we both knew it wasn't working when the final round of IVF treatment failed. After that I was to blame for everything and maybe, just maybe, she was right. I almost quit the job at one point," said Peter.

"Hey, you can't blame yourself for stuff like that," Star said as she reached out and squeezed his hand. "It just happens. It is what it is and it's out of all of our control. I'm pleased you didn't leave the force because we need good guys like you to make a difference and to support us in what we do. I know that if you were a stick of rock, it would have armed police officer written right the way through it."

"Thank you, I appreciate that. I did try to reach out to the ex-wife once the divorce was finalised, you know, to see if I could repair things or try to do something different or better so we could remain friends, but she just said that the only way she would speak to me again was through a medium," Peter said, shrugging his shoulders.

"Well, I suppose that's final then," said Star. "Are you seeing somebody else?"

"What was that? An offer to take me out?" Peter said with a forced laugh.

Star smiled and shook her head.

"I'm seeing somebody, Peter."

"I was only joking," Peter said, as he looked down at his watch. "I better get cracking. We're covering Croydon and the surrounding areas today. It's a war with all those postcode gangs."

"You take it easy out there and stay safe," Star said as she placed her empty paper coffee cup on the table.

"I will," Peter said, as he stood up and handed Star a card. "Here's my new number. Let's have a drink sometime, nothing in it, just mates letting off some steam and having a few laughs."

Star looked at the card, smiled and placed it in her handbag.

"Sure, it would be good to catch up and have a few drinks," said Star.

Star hurried along the corridor to DI Pratt's office. She began to fill him in on the Fenton kidnapping, but he was more concerned about the DC Deepika Kumar progress. He almost balked when Star showed him the estate agents vending sheet. However, after several minutes of reading and re-reading the sheet, he reluctantly agreed to speak with those above him and have an answer on the Monday. Star left the office in time for her team briefing with DC Robin Carpenter and DC Sally York.

***

"Sally you're with me. Robin, you know what to do," Star said as the team left the briefing.

"Yes Sergeant," said DC Robin Carpenter.

"Isn't the Inspector coming on this Sergeant?" asked DC Sally York.

"No, he has a meeting. I'll be keeping him posted," Star said as she opened the door to her Range Rover and placed the branded sports holdall fitted with the GPS tracking device on the back seat.

Robin followed Star in the unmarked silver BMW. They drove slowly across London's heavy traffic and finally arrived at Cheyne Walk. Star parked behind the blue Bentley and Robin parked snugly behind the Range Rover.

"Stay in the car, Sally, and keep your radio on," said Star.

"Yes, Sergeant," Sally said as she looked up at the Fenton's home admiringly. "Who says crime doesn't pay?"

"I suspect the vast majority of those villains who are in prisons up and down the country serving ten and twenty years locked up in a cell far away from their family and friends. I'm pretty sure that when the cell door is slammed shut and the light goes out, those convicts are thinking that crime doesn't pay," said Star.

"Yes Sergeant. I'm sure you're right," said Sally.

Star got out of the car. She took the sports holdall from the back seat and walked towards the gate. Star spotted the chauffeur wiping down the chrome Bentley grill. She smiled and nodded her head. The chauffeur tipped his cap. Buster had already opened the front door.

"Good morning," Star said as she entered the home.

Buster grunted and ushered her in and down the hallway. Star glanced up the stairs to where she had seen the apparition. Lady Devine wasn't there.

Shirley Fenton was already in the room. She sat by the open fireplace drinking her favourite coffee. On the coffee table was a large pile of neatly packaged twenty-pound notes.

"Good morning, Mrs Fenton," Star said as she approached the table.

"I believe it is, Detective Sergeant. I expect to have my son back home today."

"Her son, Brandon, and his alter ego Lady Devine are already dead, but I can't say anything," thought Star.

"Would you like some coffee?"

"That would be nice, thank you," Star said as she sat in the chair opposite Shirley Fenton.

"I had the strangest dream last night," Shirley said as she placed her cup on the table and looked directly at Star.

"Really?" said Star.

"Yes, and I can't for the life of me make head or tail of it," Shirley said, looking at Star intently.

*"I had a very strange dream about **you**, Mrs Shirley Fenton, but I'm not about to share those details,"* thought Star.

"I don't dream often, but when I do there seems to be some kind of message there that often makes sense in the future," Shirley said as she relaxed her glare.

"Would you like to share it with me?"

Shirley looked back abruptly and slowly smiled.

"I don't think we know each other well enough to share such intimate thoughts," Shirley said as she reached for the coffee pot and refilled her cup.

"You were dreaming about me too, weren't you? What is going on here?" thought Star.

"I think it was Sigmund Freud who said that dreams are a window into our unconscious mind. A place where we store memories, feelings and emotions that we try to supress in waking life," Shirley said before taking a sip from her coffee cup. "Hmm, this coffee never fails to deliver."

"I've never read any Freud," said Star.

"Oh, you should. His theories are fascinating. Apparently, mankind has only two drives that determine all thoughts, emotions and desires," said Shirley.

"Really, what are they?" asked Star.

"The overwhelming need for sex and aggression. After all, sex is the equivalent of life, and aggression often leads to its equivalent... death."

"That's it, just two drivers?"

"I can't believe I'm sitting here discussing the theories of Sigmund Freud with a woman who has probably had hundreds of adversaries murdered to retain the premier position amongst criminals," thought Star. *"She is a truly remarkable woman. I think I may be just a little infatuated with Mrs Shirley Fenton. No, that would crazy, wouldn't it?"*

"Once all this nasty business is over, I'll have one of Freud's books sent over to you. I have several first editions here," said Shirley.

"You seem far more relaxed today than when we last met," said Star.

"I am. The motivation behind Brandon's disappearance is money, just money. There are no bigger plans or schemes at work. If whoever it is gets away with the money then so be it, but if you're able to make arrests and bring them to justice then that would be even better. Either way I get my son back," said Shirley.

Shirley's mobile phone rang.

"It's an unknown number. It could be him," said Shirley.

The two women stood up, side by side, as Shirley pressed the button to accept and record the call.

"Mrs Fenton, do you have my money?" the kidnapper said.

"I want to talk to my son."

"No!" the kidnapper snapped. "Once I have the money your son will be released. I will not ask you again Mrs Fenton. Do you have the half a million pounds in cash?"

"Yes," Shirley Fenton replied.

"Good," the kidnapper said. "I want the money placed in a bag and dropped off at the same telephone box in Cockspur Street, Trafalgar Square, in one hour's time. Remember, we will be watching Mrs Fenton. Your son's life is in your hands!"

The kidnapper rang off.

Star reached into her handbag and pulled out her radio set. She turned up the volume and spoke.

"DC Carpenter, DC York, you know the plan. It's on," she said.

"Can I come with you?" Shirley asked.

Star shook her head.

"I'm sorry, but this is a police operation. You have to trust us to do our job. I will keep you informed, Mrs Fenton, that I will promise you," said Star.

"Call me Shirley."

Star smiled, nodded and began to fill the black branded holdall with the ransom money. The money had been bundled into ten-thousand-pound lots. Star counted all fifty bundles before zipping the bag.

"I'll call you later," she said as she lifted the sports holdall.

"Damn, this thing must weigh about 25KG!" thought Star

"Would you like Buster to help you out to the car with that, Star?" asked Shirley.

"No thank you, I'm fine," Star said, as she left the room clutching the holdall.

Once outside Star placed the holdall on the pavement, opened the car's rear door and then hoisted the holdall up onto the rear seat. She slammed the door shut and got into the driver's side.

"Is that the money, Sergeant?" Sally asked.

Star nodded and turned the ignition key.

"Imagine, half a million pounds in cash. That is a life changing amount of money."

Star ignored the comment and spoke into her radio as she pulled away.

"DC Carpenter, the drop off point is the telephone box on Cockspur Street, Trafalgar Square. Please take up your position," she said

"Yes, Sergeant. I'll be in position," came the reply.

"DC Bright. Did you get that message? Please confirm." Star said.

" Yes, Sergeant I'll be in the vicinity awaiting instructions," DC Bright replied.

Star drove over Albert Bridge.

Star said, "DC Bright I need you to be at Cardinal Place in ten minutes."

"Affirmative."

Star drove up through Euston Square and finally came to a stop next to a black London Taxi.

"Are you clear on what you have to do?" Star said as DC Sally York got out of the car.

Sally nodded.

DC Bright had followed Star's instructions and dressed as a typical London black taxi driver. He got out of the taxi and took the heavy black holdall from the back seat. Moments later Sally and the holdall were in the back of the taxi and driving away towards Saint James, Hatton Garden, and finally into Cockspur Street. Star followed at a distance and then parked about thirty metres away from the telephone box. Pretending to be a lost tourist, she took out a large map of London and put her hazard lights on.

"Robin, are you in position?" Star asked.

DC Robin Carpenter replied, "In position Sergeant."

Star peered over the map as the black taxi came to a halt by the red telephone box. She watched as Sally humped the heavy sports holdall out of the back of the cab and put it inside the telephone box. Without looking left or right, Sally got back into the taxi. Star watched as pedestrians walked back and forth without paying any attention to either the parked cars or the sports holdall. Star's attention was drawn to the sound of a large motorcycle passing her. The white Suzuki GSX-R750 stopped by the telephone box. Star read out the vehicle registration over the radio. The motorcycle had both a rider and passenger. The passenger was smartly dressed in black trousers and shoes. With his crash helmet still on, he opened the telephone box door and grabbed the black holdall.

"Everyone, get ready to move," Star said into the radio.

"Shit, why did it have to a bloody motorcycle!" she thought.

The passenger climbed back onto the motorcycle while keeping a firm grip on the holdall.

The rider revved the engine several times. He put his right indicator on and then slowly edged out into the traffic flow. Star understood from all her training that when putting a vehicle under surveillance, the initial departure from a stationary position to a mobile one was critical. The untrained would tend to leave too early and draw attention to themselves or leave the departure too late and lose the target. When following a car through busy streets, her training dictated that she should have no more than one car between her and the target.

"If they open up now the whole operation could be at risk," thought Star as she slapped the steering wheel, "I should have incorporated an undercover police motorcyclist as back up."

Despite Star's concerns the motorcycle stayed within visual distance. Her team were all well trained and kept their eyes glued to the target vehicle albeit at a safe distance. The target crossed London Bridge and turned left towards Lambeth, and headed to Vauxhall, Nine Elms, Battersea and Clapham Junction. Star followed the motorcycle into Lavender gardens where the two men parked by a black Audi S4. She watched as they removed their crash helmets. The passenger, still carrying the black holdall, used his remote to unlock the car and open the boot. The two men placed their crash helmets in the boot along with the black holdall. Star immediately read out the vehicle registration as the two men got into the car.

"Shirley Fenton said that Brandon's car was found in Clapham Junction. Is this a coincidence?" thought Star.

The team maintained surveillance across London and through Streatham towards Norbury, Thornton Heath and Croydon.

"They're heading out of London," thought Star. "This is the A23."

Star reached for her mobile phone and rang Detective Inspector Pratt's number. It went straight to voice mail.

"I need to make a decision, and fast," thought Star.

Star looked through her contacts and found Peter Eldridge's mobile number. She pressed the call button.

"Hello Star, I knew you'd call but not this quickly," Peter Eldridge said.

Not responding to his flippant comment, Star said urgently, "Peter, are you and the Trojan Proactive Unit in Croydon?"

"We are. Why, what's up?"

"I have a team following two suspected kidnappers," Star said.

She read out the vehicle description and registration number and said, "We need to bring the vehicle to a stop. Can you help?"

"Yes of course."

Star gave them their exact location.

"I suggest we stop the vehicle once we enter Hooley just before the M25," Peter said.

"Agreed, thank you," Star said.

"No problem."

Star radioed the other members of the team while they continued to follow the two suspects in the black Audi.

Star was now just two cars behind the target vehicle. As they passed through Coulsdon West the roads became a little clearer with speeds increasing to sixty miles per hour.

A white BMW sped past Star and the two cars in front and finally reached the target vehicle. Star watched as the blue neon lights began to flash. Peter and the Trojan team slowed the target vehicle down until it came to a halt on the hard shoulder. Star stopped close to the Audi's rear bumper so the target vehicle could not move. Peter and his team were all dressed in their black overalls, Kevlar helmets and were carrying sub-machine guns. Both the suspected kidnappers got out of the Audi with their hands raised.

Peter ordered both men to lie on the ground. He handcuffed one while Star handcuffed the second.

"I don't know what's going on!" pleaded the passenger. "What am I supposed to have done?"

The other man remained quiet while Star removed the black holdall carrying the ransom money from the boot of the Audi.

"You are under arrest for the kidnapping of Brandon Fenton. You do not have to say anything, but it may harm your defence if you do not mention, when questioned, something which you later rely on in court," Star said, as she helped the driver back onto his feet

"Kidnapping? You must be bloody joking! I've never even had a speeding ticket!"

"Which one of you is Aiden Sullivan? Star said, as the two men were led towards DC Robin Carpenter's parked unmarked BMW.

Star requested the names of both the motorcycle and the Audi's owner.

"That would be me. Why would the police know my name?" yelled Aiden. "I've never met a police officer in my life!"

"Then you must be Camden White," Star said. "Where are you holding Brandon Fenton?"

Camden, the driver of the black Audi, slowly closed his eyes and lowered his head.

Chapter 12

Star tried several times to provide DI Pratt with a status report. She had the two suspected kidnappers processed and placed in custody. The men were separated to avoid any collusion. Star asked Detective Constables Sally York and Robin Carpenter to interview Aiden Sullivan while she interviewed Camden White.

"Camden. That's an interesting name," Star said as she sat down.

"My mother named me after Camden Lock where I was supposed to have been conceived," Camden said as he rubbed his hands together. "Look, you have this all wrong."

"Where are you holding Brandon Fenton?" Star said firmly.

"That sounds so strange, Brandon Fenton. I think she only ever revealed her real name to me once. I've always known the man you call Brandon Fenton as Lady Devine," said Camden.

"How did you come to know Lady Devine?" asked Star.

"I've known Lady Devine now for maybe four years. We first met when she contacted me online," said Camden.

"How do you mean contacted you online?"

Camden put his hand over his mouth and chuckled.

"I'm a high-class male escort. Gentlemen, mostly married, with a colourful history of being at a public school, reward me handsomely for my company and discretion," said Camden. "You can check me out online. I have a fabulous website. Lady Devine contacted me that way.

In short, Detective Sergeant, Lady Devine loved to be fucked like a bitch and I pleasured her with all my nine-and-a-half inches."

"It would be fair to say that you were intimate?" Star said, ignoring Camden's attempt to shock her.

"Lady Devine was insatiable and just couldn't get enough of the good stuff which was why I introduced her to the Rainbow Club in Soho. Believe me, she went down a storm with the private members," said Camden. "It's a very special place where every conceivable itch can be scratched, if you get what I mean."

"So, when did you start making your plans to kidnap Lady Devine?"

Camden chuckled again and began to shake his head emphatically.

"You have all this wrong. This whole kidnapping stuff was all Lady Devine's idea."

"Pardon?" said Star.

"Yes, that's right. She had enough of living a lie. Lady Devine wanted the money so that we could both leave the country and live an open, honest life and not feel the need to lie about who and what we are."

"Camden, do you know what line of business Lady Devine's family are involved in?"

"He didn't talk much about his family only that they owned land and properties. I think he said that they were landlords or something like that. She wanted out, Detective Sergeant, away from a judgemental parent and she pleaded with me to help her. At first I declined, but we had become close, we had a lover's bond, and I could sense her pain and anguish, so eventually after a great deal of discussion about the life we could both have, I stupidly agreed," Camden said rubbing his nose.

"Gotcha!" thought Star. *"Your body language has just given you away. You're lying through your teeth Mr Camden White."*

"Where is Lady Devine now, Camden?"

Camden shrugged his shoulders.

"I just don't know. She set this whole thing up and then a few days ago she just up and left without saying a word. Everything was in motion and Lady Devine didn't say to stop so I naively carried on with her plan," said Camden.

"What was Aiden Sullivan's involvement?"

"Aiden had nothing to do with any of it. I asked him to take me into town on his motorcycle with a promise that we would spend a couple of days in Brighton and The Grand on the front. You can check the reservations if you like. They are in my name," Camden said as he leant back in his chair.

There was a loud knock on the door just before it opened, and Detective Inspector Pratt entered.

"Sir," Star said as she rose to her feet.

"A quick word, Sergeant, outside," DI Pratt muttered in a lowered tone.

"Yes sir," Star said as she followed the Inspector out into the hallway.

"I've just seen Detective Constables Carpenter and York and they're making no progress with Aiden Sullivan. How are you getting on here?"

"Camden White has confirmed that Mr Sullivan had no idea what he was involved in," said Star.

"Good I was right to let him go then," DI Pratt said as he ran his right hand through his greasy hair.

Star nodded.

"Where are you with this one?"

"White claims that the whole idea was Brandon Fenton's. Allegedly it was all part of an elaborate plan so they could leave the country and start a new life together," said Star.

"Well, I suppose half a million quid could do that. What's your take on it?"

"I think he's lying, sir."

"What evidence have you got to support your views?" DI Pratt said as he rubbed his chin.

"Very little, sir, only that we witnessed the ransom money being collected by White and we apprehended them with the money in the boot of a motor vehicle registered to White."

"That's not enough, Sergeant. So, he's claiming that Brandon Fenton faked his own kidnapping?"

Star nodded.

"Right, get a warrant issued for the arrest of Brandon Fenton, and let this White go, but make it clear that we will need to speak to him again."

"I would love to argue to keep Camden White in custody. However, seeing an apparition of Lady Devine is hardly tangible evidence. I'm going to need more," thought Star. *"Wait a minute."*

"Sir, I'd like to conduct a polygraph test on Mr White, just to be sure," Star said as she took a step back.

"You know as well as I do, Sergeant, that polygraph evidence is not admissible in a court of law," said DI Pratt as he took a step closer to Star.

"Dearie me, you need to clean your teeth or use mouth wash at the very least," thought Star.

Polygraphs are commonly known as 'lie detector' tests. They work by measuring physiological changes in the body. This can include the respiration rate, pulse, blood pressure and galvanic skin response.

"You and I know that sir, but Camden White doesn't. We've checked for previous convictions and he's clean. I'd like to try," Star said enthusiastically.

DI Pratt took a step back and rubbed his chin vigorously while looking Star up and down.

"Okay, it's contentious and wholly appropriate with registered sex offenders, but I understand you wanting to see if there's a crack we can leverage. Do it and keep me posted," DI Pratt said before turning on his heels and marching off down the hallway.

"Yes, sir," said Star.

Star had Camden White agree to a polygraph test before returning him to the cells while the forensic team set up the polygraph apparatus in the interview room. Jonathan Stevens, the polygraph expert, was called in to conduct the test. Jonathan was provided a list of background and pertinent questions by Star.

"That prison cell is freezing. You need to get some kind of heating in there," Camden said as he rubbed his hands together. "The temperature just plummeted."

"You've just been visited by Lady Devine," thought Star.

"Please, take a seat. This is Jonathan Stevens and he'll be conducting the test today.

"Fine," Camden said as he sat down.

Jonathan Stevenson prepared Camden for the test.

"We're going to start the testing now," said Jonathan. "You must only answer yes or no. Do you understand?"

Camden nodded his head.

"I need your verbal answers, Mr White. Remember, just yes or no. Is that clear?"

"Yes," replied Camden.

The apparatus moved.

"Is your name Camden White?"

"Yes."

"Have you ever used any other name for any purpose?"

"No."

"Were you born in London?"

"Yes."

"Have you ever been dismissed from any jobs you've had?"

"No."

"Do you hold a current British driving licence?"

"Yes."

"Are you a male escort?"

"Yes."

"Do you know Brandon Fenton?"

"Yes."

"Did you know Lady Devine?"

"Yes."

"Were you and Lady Devine lovers?"

"Yes." Camden said with a smirk.

"Did you and Brandon Fenton plan his kidnapping?"

"Yes."

"Did Brandon Fenton agree to fake his kidnapping?"

"Yes."

"Did you suggest five hundred thousand pounds as the ransom?"

"No."

"Have you ever been arrested?"

"No."

"Have you ever engaged in a criminal act?"

"Yes."

"Have you ever committed a serious crime?"

"No."

"Have you ever committed an undetected crime?"

"No."

"Have you ever stolen anything from a place where you have worked?"

"Yes."

"Have you any close relationships with any friends or relatives who are currently involved in criminal practices?"

"Yes."

"Have you ever sold or given drugs to another person?"

"Yes."

"Did you plan the kidnapping of Brandon Fenton?"

"No"

"Did you plan and carry out the kidnapping of Brandon Fenton?"

"No."

"Have you murdered Brandon Fenton also known as Lady Devine?"

"No!"

"Do you know where Brandon Fenton is?"

"No."

"Would you tell the police where Brandon Fenton is if you knew?"

"Yes."

"Have you answered all the questions truthfully?"

"Yes."

"Have you deliberately falsified your answers for this polygraph test?"

"No."

Jonathan Stevenson looked up to Star and indicated that the test was complete.

"Thank you," said Star.

"A cynic would look at this polygraph testing lark as a psychological prop to coerce a confession," Camden said as he rose to his feet.

"You're guilty of murdering Brandon Fenton, you nasty piece of work, and I will bring you to justice," thought Star.

Star left the table and motioned for the officer outside to take Camden back to the cells.

"Can I have a blanket please, that cell is freezing!" Camden said as he rubbed his upper arms.

"The officer will look after you," Star said as she turned her back on him.

"Jonathan, how long will you need?" Star said as she checked to see that the room was clear.

"An hour, two at the most," Jonathan said as he began to pack away the polygraph device.

"Great, I'll be in my office," said Star.

Jonathan looked down at his watch and began to shake his head.

"Okay," said Jonathan.

As Star returned to her office, she heard her mobile phone ping. She reached into her handbag and checked her phone for text messages.

'Hi Star, I'm a little too tired to go out tonight, but maybe you could pop by for a glass of wine at 9.00 pm? Julia xxx'

Star stopped in the canteen and bought a cup of coffee from the vending machine. She sat down at the table and tapped out a reply.

"Julia, that sounds wonderful. However, I can't tonight. The case I'm working on is keeping me busy. Sorry xxx'

Star pressed the send button and placed her mobile on the desk.

"I'm going to have to make time if this thing with Julia is to work. Maybe I should have stuck to one-night stands and liaisons," thought Star. *"Balancing my workload and the emotional needs of a potential partner is going to be difficult, but I know I'll have to make it work if I don't want to live alone forever."*

Star caught up with her paperwork. A little over an hour had passed when Jonathan arrived.

"Hi Jonathan, what were the results?"

Jonathan shook his head slowly.

"I'm afraid the final results are inconclusive," Jonathan said as he looked down at his watch.

"Do you have to be somewhere, Jonathan?"

"I do," said Jonathan as he straightened his tie. "It's our tenth wedding anniversary and I'm due to be at the restaurant to celebrate with my wife in fifteen minutes. If I'm lucky it'll still take twenty, maybe twenty-five minutes to get there."

"So get yourself off and enjoy your evening with your wife," Star said as she stood up and ushered him out with her hand.

Jonathan beamed, turned and raced down the corridor.

"Thank you!" Star called out after him.

Star called the custody sergeant, had Camden White released, and then text messaged DI Pratt. 'Inconclusive.'

It was almost 10.00 pm when Star stopped outside the home of Shirley Fenton. She was just about to turn her mobile phone off when she received a text message from Julia.

'I really don't know a whole lot about complicated police things, but I do believe that lovers need to care for each and protect their feelings. I'm clearly not a priority which makes me question what kind of a future we could share. I wish you well with your career. Julia'

"I know you're right, Julia, but I just don't have time for this right now," thought Star.

Star turned her mobile phone off and walked up to the front door. Buster let her in and showed her through to the study where she met with Shirley. Star described the day's events, the allegations of a fake kidnapping, and that Brandon had a secret life.

"I suppose I've always known that Brandon was different. I've suspected he was gay for, well, years. Even as a small child all the signs were there. He would love to dress up and dance for visitors when they came to the house. Neither his father, Terry, nor I would have been surprised if Brandon had made the announcement and come out of the closet, but he never did," Shirley said as she took a sip from the brandy she had poured for herself.

Star nodded.

"It doesn't add up, Star," Shirley said as she shook her head. "Brandon being gay, sure, even dressing like a woman, okay, but he doesn't need half a million pounds to start a new life. Brandon has more than five times that in personal investments and access to all the family's funds. He could cash out several million and disappear tomorrow without any of the theatrics."

"The investigation is on-going, Mrs Fenton, and I will not let it rest," Star said reassuringly.

"I appreciate your commitment and tenacity, Star," said Shirley.

***

On her way home, Star found herself thinking back to how she first decided to join the police force. She had been twelve years old and was attending a public school in Chelsea. Her fellow classmates were all from privileged backgrounds. Many formed part of the 'country' set with regular dressage or show jumping events while others attended private acting lessons so they could follow their parents into the world of show business. Star had a best friend called Tiffany. The two had become friends while attending the same primary school. They would meet up after school and play, go to the cinema in Leicester Square, or go along with Tiffany's parents to watch West End shows. Star had been careful never to reveal her gifts to anyone, not even Tiffany. Her mother told her how the Bible and most Christians strongly condemn spiritualism, mediums, psychics and the occult. She had smiled when she revealed that even those who read horoscopes, tarot cards, palm readers, astrology or fortune tellers weren't safe from Christian disdain. She emphasised over and over that her gifts must remain a secret. However, following a half term break and during a history class, Star felt the room's temperature drop suddenly so she turned around to see who had opened the window. It was then that she saw a ghostly apparition of Tiffany's mother standing behind her friend. Star found herself blurting out that she could see Tiffany's dead mother. Tiffany cried out and ran out of the class. It transpired that Tiffany's mother had died in a motor vehicle accident during the half term break. Tiffany was distraught and the revelation cost Star her friendship. Other children in her class had looked upon Star as being either simply weird or mischievous. To avoid confrontation, Star began to sit in the school library during break times and it was there that she found a magazine with an article about Irene Hughes, a powerful psychic from Chicago in America. Star read about how Irene had been making predictions around the city of Chicago since the early 1960s with many of them coming to fruition. She was particularly interested when she read how the woman had helped the police department solve a crime. The psychic had predicted that a man would be found near a large rock in the Cal-Sag Canal, dead from a gunshot in the back. Irene went on to say that the man would be wearing a white shirt and would be missing a shoe. Just as she had predicted Lt Jerry Harmon of the Cook County Sheriff's department found the dead man. Star was stunned to read that the two went on to work together, solving eight murders and one where the psychic even gave the name of the murderer. During her lifetime Irene Hughes helped police with thousands of cases. As Star sat alone in the school library, she would fantasise about joining the police when she was older and help to solve serious crimes. Tiffany's father worked with the British Government and was placed overseas, so with Tiffany gone and the start of a new year, Star found herself making a new circle of friends. She had cried when she heard that Tiffany would be leaving and there had been no reconciliation, not even a goodbye. On the one occasion that a girl asked about the previous year's events with Tiffany, she brushed it off as a simple gag to scare her friend, a joke, and that she had no idea that Tiffany had really lost her mother. How could she?

Chapter 13

"I'm feeling super excited! Thank you, Star, I truly look forward to our monthly afternoon tea at Claridges," Maude said as she stepped out of the Range Rover.

Set in the heart of Mayfair, the Claridges Hotel is an art deco icon with understated elegance. Seduced by the glamorous design, inspiring dining and impeccable service, Maude had been a regular visitor at the glamorous five-star hotel for over forty years where she had met and dined with television and movie personalities. She had once met with the King of Morocco and accepted an invitation to the Royal Palace in Casablanca. Star and Maude had been enjoying afternoon tea monthly for almost five years at one of the world's finest hotels.

"You're very welcome, Maude. I look forward to our afternoon treat," said Star.

Star and Maude were welcomed by the head doorman and shown through to the elegant art deco Thierry Despont-inspired foyer. Maude chose to sit in the main foyer. She liked to alternate between the foyer and the library. Occasionally Maude would hum along to the pianist as they played well known classics from across the musical world.

Their afternoon tea began with a selection of finger sandwiches which included chicken with lemon and tarragon on granary bread, smoked salmon with brown shrimp butter and rock samphire on rye bread, and beautiful cucumber sandwiches among others.

"The bread here is just so fluffy," Maude said as she took a nibble from her delicate sandwich. "What tea did you select?"

Star smiled.

"The same one we always start with," said Star. "The Malawi Antlers White Tea."

"Wonderful," said Maude.

The second course was Claridges famous fruit and plain scones served with clotted cream and Marco Polo Gelée which was infused with bergamot and vanilla pods. Maude chose a Darjeeling steamed tea to compliment the scones, just as she always did.

The final event included delicious choux pastries accompanied by black tea with lemongrass infusion.

"You know a pretty, nice, girl like you shouldn't be throwing her life away following a career," said Maude

"I'm happy as I am," Star said as she reached for a finger sandwich.

"When a woman reaches the tender age of thirty and she's still single and childless, people, and I mean all people, want to know why. Your family, co-workers, friends from university, the nosey neighbour and the married mums whose weddings you attended, all want to know what you're waiting for," Maude said as she poured the Earl Grey tea into the bone china cups.

Star stopped eating for a few moments.

"What is it you're waiting for, Star?"

"I've never given it any thought, Maude. However, I have no doubt that all those inquisitive people will have formed their own opinions."

"Do you not want a life partner? Somebody to share a life with and maybe have children?" Maude asked before taking a long sip from her cup.

Star paused for a few seconds.

"Yes, I would like a life partner. Somebody to come home to, share a meal and a glass of wine with, but that has eluded me. Do I want children? Maybe, I just don't know. Perhaps if I met the right man that would answer the question for me," said Star.

"The fertility clock is ticking, Star, and I would hate to see you miss the opportunity to experience being a mother."

"Thank you for reminding me, Maude," Star said, rolling her eyes.

"Is it because you have to stay competitive in your career to compete for the positions that men held previously, or do you see your career as your legacy?"

"There isn't a role in the modern police force that I couldn't do effectively as a woman so, no, I don't feel I have anything to prove to keep my job. For right now my career is an important part of who and what I am and until that changes I'll just keep on making, what I consider to be a difference."

"I wouldn't want to offend you, Star. Everything I'm saying is coming from a good place," Maude said with her broad, warm, smile.

"I know that, which is why we're such good friends," said Star.

"Almost like family," said Maude.

Star relaxed and let out a slight giggle.

"Just like family."

"This is the last I'll say on the subject, okay?"

Maude nodded.

"I'm making the choice, because it is my choice, to wait for true love, marriage and a stable relationship before making any rash decisions," Star said, as she reached for a second finger sandwich.

"A very sensible decision," Maude said with a cheeky, wry, grin.

"How has your cleaner, Tracey, been?"

"I know that Tracey is an acquired taste, but she's been surprisingly good company in recent weeks."

"Hmm, if I had a pound for every positive and upbeat thing she's ever said, I'd be poor!"

"Star, that's not like you to be sarcastic about somebody."

"I think where your cleaner is concerned, sarcasm is like punching a rude, belligerent all round nasty piece of work in the face," Star said before wiping the corners of her mouth.

"You really don't like Tracey, do you?"

"No,"

"Well, I'll have you know that she's been bringing me the most delicious 'Eton Mess'."

"Really, did she ask you for a wage increase?"

"Certainly not, well, not recently anyway," said Maude. "We had that conversation several months back when she arrived late one morning and told me that three of her other customers had all mysteriously given her a wage increase for no apparent reason. I told her, in no uncertain terms, that I already paid a higher rate and not to expect an increase from me."

"I suspect she wasn't too pleased," Star said as she sipped the last of her black tea.

Maude began to shake her head slowly then looked up and beamed.

"If looks could kill."

Star's mobile phone began to ring. She took it out of her handbag and saw that it was DC Sally York.

"I'm sorry, Maude, but I need to take this."

"Hello, Sally," Star said.

DC Sally York said "I've just been notified that a body has been found in a lock up garage in Clapham Junction. A man was out walking his dog when it started barking wildly at the garage door. The lock was broken so he entered and a found a body."

"Okay, send me over the location of the crime scene," Star replied.

"Will do. One more thing, Sergeant."

"What's that?" Star asked.

"It's a man wearing women's clothes," DC Sally York said.

"Brandon Fenton?" asked Star.

"It's not been confirmed yet," DC Sally York said.

Star said, "Let the senior officer on the crime scene know I'm on my way and it could be part of an on-going investigation."

"Will do Sergeant."

Star ended the call and placed the mobile phone back in her handbag.

"Problems at work?" asked Maude.

"Yes, I'm sorry Maude, but I'm going to have to leave," Star said, pushing her chair back and standing up.

"This is my treat today," said Maude. "You paid last month."

"Thank you. Are you okay to get a taxi back to Kensington?"

"I'm perfectly fine," Maude said with a smile. "I may even take a stroll around Harrods."

"I'll try and pop in during the next day or so," Star said, as she turned to leave.

"Star, I'll book afternoon tea for the same time and day for next month, okay?"

"Super," Star said as she stopped briefly to blow Maude a kiss.

Star sped out of Mayfair, over Battersea Bridge and into Clapham Junction. DC Sally York had messaged Star the location details. Once at the crime scene she passed by the uniformed officers and identified herself to the crime scene's senior officer. Star stepped gingerly into the derelict garage. The pungent smell of the decomposing body was overwhelming. A junior uniformed officer followed Star in and then immediately turned back and began to gag and heave violently before being sick against a graffiti covered wall. One of the more senior uniformed officers looked on briefly, shook his head slightly and carried on documenting the crime scene.

When a person dies, the body immediately begins the decomposition process and the smell of death and rotting flesh begins due to the various gases created by microorganisms.

Star looked down at the dead, bloated body. There were several bullet wounds and severe head injuries visible.

She took out her phone and looked back through the images she had taken during the investigation. When she came across the photograph she had taken at the Rainbow club, she knew that it was Brandon Fenton also known as Lady Devine.

Star stepped outside back into the daylight and phoned DC Sally York.

"Hello Sally, this is now a murder investigation." Star said. "I want forensics to go over his clothing looking for fibres and do DNA testing."

"Yes, Sergeant," DC York said.

Star said, "I'll be in my office shortly."

"Sergeant have you seen or spoken with Robin? Sorry, I mean Detective Constable Robin Carpenter?" DC York asked Star.

"Not recently, why?"

DC Sally York said, "He hasn't been himself since yesterday morning. It's like something is really playing on his mind. I did try talking with him, but he just clammed up tight. I thought maybe you should know."

"I'll speak with him later. Thank you for bringing that to my attention," Star said.

Star got back into her Range Rover. Her mobile phone pinged just as Star was about to start the engine. She reached down and read the message from Detective Inspector Pratt.

'DC Kumar's demands agreed subject to a signed NDA'

"Wow, I didn't expect that!" thought Star. *"There has to be some pretty serious backside covering here. I wonder what kind of spin DI Pratt has put on it to pull that off."*

Star looked up Deepika's mobile number and selected "Call". The phone answered on the fourth ring.

"Hello Deepika, its Detective Sergeant Star Bellamy," she said.

DC Deepika Kumar replied, "Hello Sergeant, how are you?"

"Busy as always. What about you?"

"I'm sitting in the garden with a glass of freshly squeezed orange juice looking online for inspiration as to what I'll be doing next in life," DC Kumar said.

"The freshly squeezed orange juice sounds fabulous," Star said.

"I have a full jug if you'd like to join me."

"That's very kind, but I'm chasing my tail at the moment," Star replied

"Oh well, another time, maybe?" DC Kumar said.

"That would be nice."

"I can't imagine you making a social call in the middle of an investigation which means that you must have some news for me," DC Kumar said.

"I have, Deepika. Detective Inspector Pratt has authorised me to advise you that the Metropolitan Police have agreed to your compromise proposal subject to you signing an NDA, a Non-Disclosure Agreement."

"Fine," DC Kumar replied. "Do you want me to come in, will it be emailed, it or will you bring it yourself?"

"It will be emailed, Deepika. Are you okay? You don't sound pleased about the outcome."

"It feels like an empty victory, Star. This is it now, no more police work and I'm sitting here thinking about what else can I do," DC Kumar said.

"I'm sorry things turned out as they have. You're a bright, intelligent woman who will add value and make a difference wherever you choose to work," Star said.

"That's very kind."

Star looked down at her watch.

"I wish you all the best in whatever you choose to do," Star said

DC Deepika Kumar said, "A few months back DC Sally York confided in me that an officer made a series of inappropriate, suggestive, comments. It's not really for me to say but I feel that as Sally is an integral part of your team, I needed to make you aware."

"I appreciate you sharing that with me, Deepika."

"Sally must never know that it came from me," DC Kumar replied

I will be extremely tactful if and when I broach the subject with Sally," Star replied

"I'm saddened that it has come to this," DC Kumar said. "I wish you and your team all the very best of luck for the future."

"Thank you."

"Take care, Star and thank you."

Detective Constable Deepika Kumar hung up.

"What a waste of a damn fine police officer!" thought Star.

Star returned to the police station. She wrote up her notes and then asked DC Robin Carpenter to come into her office.

"Yes Sergeant?" DC Robin Carpenter said as he stood awkwardly by the open door.

"Come in and close the door please," said Star.

DC Robin Carpenter closed the office door and walked hesitantly towards Star's desk.

"Robin, are you okay? You don't seem to be your normal self," Star said as she motioned Robin to take a seat.

"Yes Sergeant,"

"Really?" Star said as she looked quizzically at him.

"Well, maybe not," DC Robin Carpenter said as he relaxed in the chair.

Star motioned him to tell her more.

"I've had this strange and to be honest, quite frightening experience and it's shaken me to the core," said Robin.

"Is it work related?"

Robin shook his head.

"Do you want to share it with me?" said Star.

"It sounds crazy when you say it out loud," said Robin.

"Try me," said Star.

"Okay, but it's pretty damn spooky," Robin said as he relaxed into his chair. "As you probably know, Sergeant, I'm a big fan of rugby and generally go to a game every other week with friends from my uni days. We tend to make a bit of a day of it, you know starting off early in a pub somewhere before the game and then celebrating the win or loss after. It can get a little boozy but that's all part of the rugby day out ritual. My girlfriend, Vikki, isn't a fan of rugby and doesn't like me to drink too much. On most things we will find some kind of compromise to keep the relationship on track, but I categorically draw the line when it comes to meeting with the boys and having our day out at rugby. Now normally Vikki will kick up a bit of a fuss but when she sees that I'm not budging she'll just get the hump and maybe not speak to me for a day or two. I know that is not an ideal situation, but I've learnt to live with it."

"Okay," Star said, leaning forward.

"Well, this time she was almost pleading with me not to go. At first I thought it was just a change in tactics to get her own way, so I remained stubborn. Even when the tears came, I remained firm. I was going out with mates whether she liked it or not. I saw it as my little piece of independence being taken away and I wasn't ready to become another go to work and pay the bills drone. It was only when I came to put on my coat that I felt this overwhelming need to step back and reconsider everything. I battled with myself for several minutes but in the end, I slipped off my jacket and gave my boozy day out with the boys a miss. It was the first time I had ever succumbed, but it was like I said, Sergeant, these were pleas rather than demands. I stayed at home. I won't pretend that I was happy with my decision. It was only when I received a phone call from a friend the next day that the enormity of everything hit me."

"What hit you, Robin."

"My friend told me all the boys had been driving along a country road when a near miss from a car overtaking on the other side of the road forced them to crash into a four-foot-deep ditch. The car burst into flames, and they were unable to open the doors because the car was jammed tight. Members of the public tried to help, but the flames beat them back."

"I'm so sorry," said Star.

"Every one of them died. I still can't believe it, the boys are all dead and had Vikki not pleaded with me not to go, I would have been in that car too. That split decision while putting on my jacket meant that I'm still alive today. It's scary when you realise just how fragile life can be and nobody knows what tomorrow will bring."

"I'm so sorry for the loss of your friends Robin," Star said, as she lowered her head. "Did you speak to Vikki about it?"

"We spoke about it at length last night Sergeant. All she could say was that she had this powerful feeling that she had to stop me from going at all costs. How can something like that happen?"

"Maybe it just wasn't your time yet," said Star.

"Really? Do you believe in stuff like that, Sergeant?"

"I believe there's a lot more to this life than the paper thin veneer we live on," said Star.

"Well, I'll be listening to everything Vikki has to say now."

"But didn't you say you also had a feeling you should just stay at home?"

"Yes, I did."

"Then maybe you could learn to understand and trust those instincts," said Star.

"I will, Sergeant, and thank you for listening."

"No problem, Robin. My door is always open for both work and personal issues. If I can help, even by just listening, I will," said Star.

"I appreciate that, Sergeant. I would prefer it, if, well you know," Robin said awkwardly.

"What?"

"You know, that we keep this kind of spooky stuff just between you and I."

Star grinned.

"Whatever you say in here, stays in here."

Robin stood up to leave.

"Can you leave the door open on your way out, please?" Star said as she reached for her mobile phone.

"I want to tell Shirley Fenton that we've found her son, but I know I can't until the forensics team confirm that it is Brandon's body," thought Star. *"Head of the criminal premier league or not, the poor woman must be going through hell not knowing what's happened to her son."*

Chapter 14

It was after 10.30 when Star finally arrived home from a late night in the office catching up on reports and sifting through the evidence relating to the murder of Brandon Fenton and his secret life as Lady Devine. She had phoned ahead to a local Chinese take-away which she collected on her way home to Kensington. She slipped off her high heels, took out an opened bottle of chilled Chardonnay from the fridge and filled a glass. Once she had eaten her Singapore Fried Noodles, she took her glass of wine through to the lounge, sat back in her armchair and took a long sip from the glass. She closed her eyes and began to think back to her early days as a Detective Constable and her memories of the notorious, charismatic Detective Inspector Richie Baker.

"Hey, Detective Constable Bellamy, what's the story, morning glory?" DI Richie Baker said with a broad grin.

"I'm just excited and ready to go, sir," Star said as she packed away the file on her desk.

Star had been selected to work with a team led by DI Richie Baker. Her extensive training gave her an insight into what a police officer does. Star understood that the primary objective was not just to reduce crime by utilising cutting edge technology and solid teamwork, but to reduce the public's fear of crime by working with local communities and establishing a reassuring presence. It was the first time she had hands on experience working a case. Star had excelled at providing background research and managing up to a very hands-on dissenter and non-conformist senior officer. He had often joked with the team that the bureaucratic pen pushers upstairs hated him and all he stood for with a vengeance, but they knew he would get the job done and put the bad guys away. In the increasingly modern police force Detective Inspector Richie Baker's behaviour and practices, despite only being in his early forties, were considered an outlandish throwback to the 1970s.

"Right, team, listen up," said DI Richie Baker.

The team of six all sat up behind their desks.

"I don't doubt, even for a minute, that you have all read through the files and acquainted yourselves fully with this case, but I'm going to bring you up to speed anyway," DI Baker said before taking a deep breath. "We have had an undercover operative on the Glyndon Estate in Plumstead for almost three years. Our man has had to put up with some serious shit which will never make the official reports, but he's trusted and accepted amongst the heavy hitters. He's known as Big Jay and has been instrumental in bringing down a gun running firm. He has also played a major part in providing evidence which led to the conviction of members of the Romanian Albescu family. They specialised in human trafficking, having sold several hundred immigrants into forced labour, sexual slavery and sexual exploitation. Mrs Elana Albescu was recorded as saying that the family preferred to trade in people over drugs as they could be sold over and over and if they didn't comply, then they would extract their organs or tissues and sell them on the black market. These were nine carat nasty pieces of work and Big Jay provided what was needed to bring them to task. He's a good man doing an extremely dangerous job. He's not as handsome as me but a good guy all the same."

There were smiles and chuckles as DI Baker began to move amongst their desks.

"This operation is to take down the 'BMB' also known as the 'Big Money Boys. This scumbag crew has moved up the criminal underworld ladder from aggravated burglaries, stabbings of rival gangs and taxing independent drug dealers, to forging a partnership with a firm of Russian heavy hitters. We have very little on the Russians, only that they're politically connected and have been moving serious weight into some of London's postcode gangs. Big Jay has been firming up the evidence and we have them on conspiracy to murder, murder and the distribution of Class A narcotics. We have strong intelligence that puts the Russians and the BMB together today doing a drug deal. These are violent career criminals and it's just us that stands between them and a very long stretch inside prison, so understand that they will be carrying weapons and they will, almost certainly, use them," DI Baker said as he stretched and cracked his fingers.

"Detective Constable Bellamy," DI Baker said as he stopped and looked directly at Star.

"Yes, sir," said Star.

"You're with me on this one. It's about time we got you moved out from behind that desk," DI Baker said with a wry grin.

"Yes, sir. Thank you, sir," Star said as she stood up and pushed her chair firmly into the desk space.

"Good," DI Baker said as he looked down at his wristwatch. "We're on the move in ten minutes, be ready!"

Star sat in the back of the unmarked police car while DI Baker's Sergeant sat beside him. DS John Holmes was a thoroughly modern police officer. The relationship between him and his superior was often strained with short, frustrated, outbursts from DS Holmes, which would be batted away with wit and sarcasm.

DI Baker turned the car stereo on. *'Supersonic'* by Oasis blasted out of the speakers.

"Really, sir? Do we really need this on?" DS Holmes asked as he strapped his seat belt on.

DI Baker began to bob his head back and forth to the beat. He turned, smiled and winked at Star.

"One day, John, you'll be the top dog with your own team, but right now you're with me whether you like it or not, so sit back and enjoy the ride. Besides," DI Baker said with a sarcastic chuckle, "What kind of man doesn't like Oasis?"

DI Baker turned the music down once the track had finished and called in on the police radio to ensure that everyone was in their positions. He undid his seat belt and turned to Star.

"There is more to this than just arresting a drug dealer, DC Bellamy. With the kind of weight our intelligence tells us the Russians are giving them on loan puts the BMB into the major league, which will almost certainly mean that they will want to expand into Woolwich, Abbey Wood and possibly New Cross and beyond. There will be blood and carnage on the streets as they fight for territory and the right to sell their new supply line. Derrell Anderson is the leader of the BMB, and his name is synonymous with extreme violence. We have to take him down before the body count goes up as he consolidates his position and territory. He is not to be underestimated because the man is no typical street thug with just a dream to escape the life of social housing he was born into. Derrell Anderson is educated, hungry for power and has no moral boundaries," said DI Baker. "That makes him, potentially, an extremely dangerous criminal."

"Yes, sir." said Star.

The officers took up their positions. At exactly 3.00 pm five scooters and a blue BMW M3 arrived and parked by the entrance to a block of flats.

"See that, Star?" DI Baker said as he pointed to the scooters. "That's how the bastards are transporting the drugs around to customers, distribution points and how they're evading the police on the ground.

If you give chase in a car, they can lose you in minutes by scooting up alleyways or riding on the pavements. Big Jay tells me that Derrell Anderson has gone all green and has been out buying eScooters. Can you believe it? It transpires that he plans to give the electric scooters away free to youngsters in a bid to bring them into his distribution network."

"Do you think we should be more pro-active with our patrolling and stop more scooters, DI Baker?" said Star.

"You would like to think so," said DI Baker. "As police officers we have the right to ask their name, what they're doing in the area and where they are going. But, and this is the kicker, they do not have to answer any questions and that alone isn't enough to search them, the vehicle or make an arrest. You must have reasonable grounds to suspect that they're carrying illegal drugs, weapons, stolen property or in the case of the BMB during the early days, a crowbar that could be used to commit a crime. If you do enough stop-and-searches without results, the officer can find himself in trouble for police harassment, racism and the list goes on. There are days, DC Bellamy, when I think we're almost at war with ourselves and I fear very much for the future."

Star nodded.

"Hold up," DI Baker said. "Now what do we have here?"

A black luxury cross-over SUV BMW X5 stopped by the parked scooters. Star watched as the lads, still wearing their crash helmets gathered around the back of the BMW's tailgate. DI Baker reached for the police radio.

"The Russians are in town, be ready to move when I give the order," DI Baker said as he stared intently out of the side window.

A huge man wearing a black suit got out from the front of the BMW X5 and opened the rear door of the car. Another man got out. He wore a white open neck shirt with black trousers. His hair was grey and styled into a side parting.

"That must be the Russian," said DS Holmes.

"Nothing gets by you," DI Baker said sarcastically as he slowly shook his head. "I suppose the big fella must be his bodyguard."

DS Holmes said nothing but kept his eyes firmly on the suspected drug deal.

The door of the blue BMW M3 finally opened and a young, well-dressed man, in designer blue jeans, Polo shirt and Gucci trainers got out.

"Do you think that might be Derrell Anderson, John?" DI Baker said, still shaking his head.

DI Baker reached for the police radio while he watched the suspected Russian and Derrell Anderson as they slowly approached each other. Derrell held out his hand and the Russian shook it vigorously. They chatted while walking to the back of the BMW X5. The bodyguard opened the tailgate.

"Go, go, go!" DI Baker yelled down the police radio.

Three unmarked police cars sped into position. DI Baker slammed his vehicle into first gear and dropped the clutch while planting his foot down hard on the accelerator. The tyres squealed as they struggled to grip the tarmac. Thick grey smoke belched out from the rear wheel arches as the car slid sideways, leaving thick black tyre marks on the road. DI Baker slammed the gear stick into second and pulled the steering wheel sharply to the right. The car came to an abrupt halt. The lads around the back of the tailgate scattered and ran back to their scooters.

"Stop, armed police," DI Baker yelled out.

Even as the police moved in, the criminals continued to scatter. One of the scooters was riding at full speed towards the alleyway that DI Baker had sealed with his driving. Instinctively Star opened her door and pushed it wide open just as the rider tried to make his way through the small gap. The door took the full brunt of the impact with the rider flying over the scooter's handlebars and landing in a heap on the hard concrete. With her adrenalin pumping, Star raced towards that take down. The Russian bodyguard produced a semi-automatic firearm from under his jacket. DS Holmes discharged his weapon. Three shots were fired, the bodyguard dropped his weapon and collapsed onto one knee. The lead Russian immediately put his hands in the air. As DS Holmes approached him, he kept his weapon firmly fixed on the target. Another officer had run and thrown himself onto the escaping scooter rider. The pair landed clumsily on the tarmac. Within seconds the officer had the rider's hands up behind his back and was handcuffing him. Derrell Anderson ignored the warning and made a run for it. He knocked over a uniformed officer and then slid across the bonnet of an unmarked police car. He bolted away, turning briefly to see that DI Baker was in hot pursuit. Star followed her superior officer. Derrell ducked into the archway which led through to a play park. It was empty. DI Baker puffed and panted and forced every ounce of strength to keep pace with his target. Derrell attempted to leap clean over the entrance gate but fell awkwardly to the ground as it shot open and sent him off balance. DI Baker was now almost upon him. Seeing his target fall had released a second burst of energy. Derrell was back up on his feet but was limping. Now just a few inches behind him, DI Baker reached out to grab Derrell Anderson's shoulder. Derrell turned quickly and managed to knock Richie off balance. He ripped his trousers and had torn the skin off his knees. Derrell, while puffing and panting, lifted his polo shirt and produced a handgun. Richie sighed and shook his head as he slowly got back onto his feet. He rubbed away the dirt marks on his trousers and then stood upright. Derrell was wide eyed and had the gun aimed at Richie.

"Come on Derrell. It's all over son," said DI Baker.

"You fucking Feds, you ain't flipping no game here, bruv," Derrell said as he gasped for breath.

"We've got you bang to rights, son. The best thing you can do now is just fall into the system and we'll both play the game out. You know, just as I do, how all this works," said DI Baker.

"I ain't going nowhere bruv, I have a destiny to play out and doing a stretch in the scrubs ain't no part of it. Just take it easy geez, get smart, turn your back and walk away. I don't want to cap you bruv but I will," Derrell said as he nodded his head and raised the gun.

"Not on my watch," DI Baker said as he took one small step towards Derrell.

BANG!

Richie grabbed his chest.

BANG! BANG! BANG!

Detective Inspector Richie Baker fell to the ground in a pool of blood.

Star had seen the conversation between the two men and had made her way around the park while keeping out of sight. As Derrell fired and her superior fell to the ground, she almost let out a yell of horror but didn't. Star raced across the grass and threw herself into one of Jiu Jitsu's most inherently dangerous moves, the flying submission. As Derrell turned, still armed, he faced Star steaming towards at him at full speed. As he raised the gun, Star knocked his right arm with a left-handed block, buried her head into his neck and shoulder while grabbing the back of his neck with her right hand. Within the same rapid movement, she pulled weight down on his left and then leapt into the air and placed her legs either side of his right arm. Derrell dropped the weapon as she fell backwards pulling him down onto the ground with the back of her knee and holding him in a choking position while, with both hands, she pulled on his right arm. Derrell spluttered and coughed but couldn't move or say anything. Star held him while he choked and struggled for breath. She looked over at the motionless body of her superior officer, Detective Inspector Baker.

"DC Bellamy, it's okay, you can let him go," DS Holmes said as he aimed his firearm at Derrell Anderson. Star let go of her grip, rolled backwards and got back onto her feet. A second officer turned Derrell Anderson over, thrust his arms behind his back and handcuffed him."

"Derrell Anderson, you're under arrest." DS Holmes said. "Now get a bloody ambulance here!"

Star walked over to the limp body. She dropped down onto one knee and placed her finger on his neck to check Richie's pulse. When she felt nothing, she looked up at DS Holmes and shook her head.

The operation, it was generally felt, was a success, with several long prison sentences administered. Derrell Anderson was sentenced to life imprisonment without parole for murder. Detective Sergeant Holmes was promoted to Detective Inspector and Star was seconded to another team.

Star opened her eyes and looked up at the crystal cut chandelier.

"I do miss you, DI Richie Baker and wish you well wherever you are," thought Star.

"Today's police force was never going to be for you. Believe me, if you were still here, you'd either hate every day or you would have been pensioned off early."

Star yawned as she wandered down the hallway into her bedroom. She slipped out of her clothes and slid into her comfy queen size bed, reached over to her mobile phone and set the alarm for 6.00 am.

Chapter 15

Star was sitting in the police canteen having a coffee with Detective Sergeant Kyle Attwood from East London. The two had met while being seconded to a task force to infiltrate and bring an Albanian gang to justice. It was after the successful operation that Star was promoted to Detective Sergeant under DI Ronald Pratt.

"The media would have everyone believe that knife crime was the most significant challenge facing the police today, but you and I both know they're wrong," DS Attwood said as he sipped his coffee.

Star nodded and blew on her hot coffee.

"Sure, knife crime, as in carrying a weapon, is on the increase with postcode gang warfare, but actual murders or violent assaults caused by knife crime has fallen. But I suppose that just doesn't sell newspapers," said DS Kyle Attwood.

"One could almost believe that someone, somewhere, is playing a game of misdirection," said Star. "Violent crimes may well have fallen but the more complex, serious and organised crimes like drug smuggling, human trafficking and sexual crimes against children are on the rise," Star said as she put her coffee cup on the table.

"Don't even get me started on crimes against children. We all know who is responsible and where they are, but those above us are too afraid to tackle the problem head on for fear of losing their jobs or by being labelled. The left are very good with labels and peer pressure," said DS Attwood.

"This is a touchy subject," Star said as she scanned the room.

"Yeah, I know but it just makes me angry. I joined the police force to take out the bad guys, not pussy foot around the guilty who are being heavily protected by left wing do-gooders," DS Attwood said, lowering his voice.

"This is modern policing," Star said, shrugging her shoulders.

"All I can say is it's no wonder we're failing to attract recruits and retain those that do make the leap of faith," DS Attwood said in the same lowered tone.

"I think that even the government is now having to rethink policing as a whole. The serious crimes cross many of the forty-three territorial police forces operating in England and Wales. It will need some serious restructuring to tackle organised crime," said Star.

"The government recognising the scale of the problem and actually doing something about it is a whole different thing," DS Attwood said, as he slowly shook his head. "Unless it grabs the headlines of course."

"I have faith that change will come," Star said, as she straightened her posture and smiled.

"Hope you're right, Star. I really do."

"Have you heard from anyone from the Hellbanianz operation?" Star said as she finally took a sip of her piping hot coffee.

The Hellbanianz were street dealers and enforcers in East London. The task force had identified them as the retail distribution arm of the Mafia Shqiptare. The Albanian crime syndicate were attempting to consolidate power in the UK criminal underworld and take over the five-billion-pound cocaine market. The operation was being led by one man, Altin Dervishi who became known simply as 'Goldie' and was considered by many as a mafia maverick. Goldie had developed strong relationships with the Columbian cartels and bypassed the existing drug import, wholesale and street distribution model. With tried, trusted and proven logistics in place, Goldie began to negotiate directly with the Columbian cartels who controlled South American coca production. Large shipments entered the UK priced at five thousand pounds per kilo at a time when the Dutch wholesalers were demanding twenty-four thousand pounds per kilo. Goldie lowered the market price of cocaine, increased its purity and rapidly grew his market share, leaving the traditional criminal gangs unable to compete. In addition to his business savvy, Goldie was known to be utterly ruthless when protecting his business interests.

Intelligence suggested the Fenton Firm, headed by Shirley Fenton, invited Goldie to negotiate a compromise. He responded with an alleged assassination attempt on her life which resulted in the death of one of her minders. When it failed, he was given a second opportunity to negotiate a compromise. However, when he refused, Goldie and his trusted lieutenants mysteriously disappeared overnight. Their bodies were never found. Police Intelligence suggested that Shirley Fenton had claimed the Albanian ancestral code of the 'Kanun' - blood for blood - which was the right to take revenge, and had negotiated a sophisticated win/win deal with both the Albanian and Italian crime syndicates. The Hellbanianz operation concluded with several street dealers, enforcers and local gang leaders being arrested and convicted and the criminal status quo being restored.

"I have actually. Do you remember Tom, Tom Parker?" said DS Attwood.

"Yes, I do," Star said with a broad smile. "He was a detective constable like us back then. Nice guy as I remember, with a great sense of humour."

"I think he liked you," DS Attwood said with a chuckle.

Star blushed and looked away momentarily.

"He was a nice guy but not my type," Star said with a wry smile. "Anyway, how is he?"

"It's been a bloody nightmare for him," said DS Attwood.

"Why, what's happened?"

"He got called out on a domestic, the usual, husband and wife going hammer and tongs on the estate after a late session in the pub. The neighbours had called in the screaming and Tom was the first to arrive. He could hear the yelling and shouting inside the flat, so he knocked on the door announcing that he was the police and to open up. He was told to fuck off and mind his own business. Tom knocked again, respectfully asking that the door be opened. It opened, and a six-foot-five monster of a man filled the doorway. Tom saw that the man's white shirt had blood on it, and he could hear a woman whimpering, so he pushed past fearing that she may need medical attention. As Tom entered the living room, he found the woman lying on the floor curled in a ball. Her face was red and swollen. She had clearly been assaulted. When Tom reached for his radio to call for an ambulance the man knocked it out of his hand and took up some kind of boxing stance. As he threw a right jab Tom used his training and brought the man down. As he fell to the floor, he caught his face on the corner of the coffee table. Tom handcuffed him and held him until back up arrived. The wife was taken to hospital and treated for multiple cuts and bruises. The husband called in a lawyer, as is his right, and within hours Tom found himself being accused of using excessive force and for making racist remarks," said DS Kyle Attwood.

"That's terrible," Star said with a shocked expression.

"That's not all though. It has been suggested that the use of force to bring a man twice his size down was not proportionate or reasonable in the circumstance and therefore unlawful. The wife, now out of hospital and all loved up again has signed a statement saying that Tom used racist and abusive, language and attacked her husband. So, while

Tom is sitting at home thinking about his future and possible criminal proceedings, the husband and wife, with advice from their solicitor, have launched a lawsuit against the police force. So, you know where all this is going, don't you?"

Star nodded her head in disbelief.

"Tom will be the sacrificial lamb and the husband and wife will get an out of court settlement," said DS Attwood.

"I'm stunned," said Star.

"This is your modern police force, Star, and I have to tell you, after that I'm now seriously considering what I want for the future because that could happen to any one of us at any time. Each and every day we, as police officers, put ourselves on the front line in the belief we're making a difference but now I'm questioning. What is it all for?" said DS Attwood.

Star thought for a few moments and then placed her empty coffee cup in the bin beside the table.

"We *are* making a difference, Kyle. There are hundreds, if not thousands of people who are still alive because of the job we do. We are that thick blue line, and we need educated, tenacious officers like you to help drive through the changes the police force so desperately needs," Star said as she stood up.

"I suppose so, but it does make you think," said DS Attwood.

"Yes, it does, but not for too long," Star answered with a grin.

"Anyway, it was good to see you again, Star. Maybe when you have some time pop over to East London and have a few drinks," DS Attwood said as he stood up.

"I just may do that. You take care," Star said as she shook Kyle's hand.

"You too."

Star made her way back to her office. No sooner had she sat down than DC Robin Carpenter knocked on the open door.

"Robin, come in," said Star.

"Sergeant we've heard back from forensics," Robin said, waving two sheets of paper.

"What do we know?"

"There were six bullet wounds, one of which entered the heart. Brandon Fenton would have died instantly, Sergeant," Robin said as he read from the documents.

"Anything else?"

"Mr Fenton had significant head injuries which are believed to have been caused by the handle of a large handgun. It was a vicious, bloody murder Sergeant," said Robin.

"What did the entomologist report?"

Robin raised the paperwork and read through it again.

"The time of death was before Mr Fenton was reported as being kidnapped," said Robin.

"Okay, if there's anything else keep me posted," Star said as she opened her email and began to write a status report to DI Pratt. Once Star had finished the email, she gathered up her coat and closed her office door behind her.

"I'm going to Mrs Shirley Fenton to inform of her of her son's murder. I'll keep my phone on, if you need me," Star said as she began to walk through the office.

"Sergeant," called Sally.

"Yes, Sally," Star said as she quickly gazed down at her watch.

"Would you like some back up or company?"

Star smiled.

"Thank you, I'll be fine."

The traditional rush hour traffic allowed Star to rehearse what she would say and how she would deliver it. Her mind raced as she walked herself through all the possible scenarios. She concluded that it was a job that had to be done and that she was best placed to do it.

It was dusk when Star arrived at the Fenton's home in Cheyne walk. She parked her black Range Rover and walked up towards the front door. Star's mind insisted on playing out each and every scenario again and again. The front door opened, and Buster beckoned her in. He led her to the study where she had met with the family's matriarch before. Shirley was standing by the open fireplace with her hands behind her back.

"Good evening, Mrs Fenton," Star said as she came to a halt by the chesterfield settee.

Shirley Fenton raised her head slowly until her eyes met Star's.

"That's just it, isn't it?" said Shirley. "It's not a good evening. In fact, it will probably be remembered as one of the worst evenings of my life."

Star remained silent.

"You're here to tell me that you've found my son, aren't you?"

Star nodded.

"He's been murdered, hasn't he?"

"We found a body matching the description of your son, Brandon Fenton. I'm very sorry for your loss Mrs Fenton," Star said in a quiet, sincere, tone.

"Only a mother would know what it's like to lose a child, Star," said Shirley. "I need you to find the man responsible."

Star nodded.

"We will do everything in our power to find your son's killer."

"Right," Shirley Fenton said as she rubbed her hands together. "If there's nothing else, I have a business meeting shortly and I'll need to prepare."

"Okay," Star said with a quizzical tone.

"Please keep me posted," Shirley Fenton said with a firm, business-like response.

"I will."

Star was shown back down the hallway by Buster where she passed three men of Eastern European origin. She turned quickly and caught a brief glimpse of Lady Devine's apparition at the top of the stairs.

Chapter 16

Star had a restless night. She woke several times and struggled to get back to sleep. She found herself thinking back to the days when her mother would talk to her about her psychic and medium gifts. Star could see and hear her mother telling her how she would need those abilities one day for a greater purpose. When questioned she would always respond with a smile and the words 'all in good time.'

Star could feel the temperature in the room falling. It disturbed her thoughts and then, as she began to turn onto her side, she caught sight of a figure standing by the bed. Instinctively Star sat bolt upright and pushed herself away from the bedside.

Before her was an apparition of the soldier in full combat uniform.

"I did not invite you and I have no time," Star said firmly.

"I was a young man. I died, but not in the line of duty. My life was not theirs to take. I have been robbed of all my tomorrows"

Star could feel a tremendous sadness from the apparition.

"I'm afraid."

Star sat up in bed and faced the soldier.

"What are you afraid of?"

"I'm afraid of what happens next."

While the soldier did not speak out loud, she could hear his words clearly in her mind.

"What is your name, soldier?" said Star.

"Private Stanley Wilkins."

"Where were you killed, Stanley?"

"I was in Dunkirk with the 2nd Battalion of the Royal Norfolk Regiment. We were outnumbered by the Germans. There was no choice but to surrender. My friends and I were marched to a farm in Le Paradis. We were ordered at gun point, to climb into a pit. It was then that I heard the sound of machine gun fire and found myself lost. I was no longer alive and afraid of what was to come."

"That was the second World War, Stanley," said Star.

"Did we win?"

"We won the war. Stanley, with our American Allies but it took another five years," said Star.

"Five years, I have been nowhere for five years?"

"Stanley, the second world war ended almost seventy-five years ago," said Star.

"You are not alone though Stanley. Everybody wants to know what happens when we die, and the journey will be different for us all."

"I don't want to be here any longer and I'm afraid of what's next."

"In the transition of death, Stanley, we all leave our physical bodies behind. I would imagine that your body is with your fellow brothers in arms at Dunkirk but your spirit, your very essence, the pure being of who you actually are, continues. That is why you are here, right now," said Star. "Your journey must continue, as it is the evolution and development of your soul. Death is not the end but the beginning of a new stage.

Star stopped to take a breath.

"Have you felt that loved ones were around you after you died, Stanley?" asked Star.

"I was confused and escaped the light."

"When the time is right and you see the light, you will be met by friends, family and loved ones. It was your traumatic ending that has kept you in this holding place. Your spirit needed to rest and recuperate after your life in this realm but your time to pass over will come soon. Your loved ones will help you to review your time here and understand what lessons you have learnt."

"I think I may be ready to pass over."

The soldier held out his hand. In the corner of the bedroom a bright, warm, light began to slowly appear. As it got bigger, Star could make out the outlines of figures within the light.

"Doris? Is that you Doris?"

Star watched as the soldier's apparition moved gingerly towards the light.

"I love you Doris, I have always loved you my beautiful wife, my soul mate."

"I wish you strength to face the next part of your journey, Stanley. May you find love, joy and happiness in the next realm," Star said, a tear trickling down her cheek.

Star watched as Stanley entered the light. He was surrounded by familiar figures that embraced him fully. She could feel an intense sense of love and warmth emanating from the light. Stanley turned, smiled and waved as the light faded away.

Star looked at the clock on her bedside cabinet. It was 5.15 am and light was just beginning to fill the bedroom. The psychic experiences Star had encountered throughout her life always left her incredibly hungry. Star turned off the alarm, showered and got dressed. Within thirty minutes she was in her Range Rover and driving across London to the Regency Café in Westminster. Like many Londoners, Star looked upon the Regency Café as serving the best, no frills, traditional English breakfast in all of London. It had been serving breakfasts since 1946 and had retained all its post-war charm with red chequered curtains and Formica tables. It was Star's mother who had first taken her there when she was a little girl. She remembered how very different it was to the venues her mother usually attended. She would smile as she parked the car outside the café and say you should never judge a book by its cover.

Star finished her breakfast and put the cutlery neatly on the plate. As she drank tea from a huge white ceramic mug, she reflected on what a beautiful experience it had been, assisting Stanley, the soldier, to pass onto the next stage of his existence.

Star was in her office before everyone else. She was reading through her notes on the murder of Brandon Fenton before turning on her emails. The last email confirmed that she had obtained a warrant to search the murder suspect, Camden White's, BMW. She had, in anticipation, contacted the forensic officer to be ready to move quickly once it had been approved. Through the open office door, she spotted Robin and Sally entering the office. They were both carrying paper cups of coffee.

"Robin, Sally can you come here please?" Star said as she closed her laptop.

"Yes, Sergeant."

"Good morning, Sergeant," said Sally.

"Good morning to you both. I need you, Robin to go to Mr Camden White's home address and bring him in for further questioning."

"Okay, is there a particular line of enquiry you want me to pursue, Sergeant?" said Robin.

"No, just go over what we have already asked," said Star.

Robin had a quizzical expression.

"Is there any reason why, Sergeant?"

"Yes, Sally, a forensic team and I will be going through Camden White's car with a fine tooth comb. We have the warrant. I need you to haul him out of bed by 9.00 am. The team and I will swoop in shortly afterwards. Any questions?" Star said as she looked at both members of her team intently.

"No Sergeant."

"Nice one Sergeant," Robin said with a broad smile. He turned and quickly bounded out of the office.

"Have you got time for a quick coffee, Sergeant?" said Sally.

Star paused for a moment.

"Only if it's because we need to need to talk about something," Star said as she looked up at Sally.

Sally shook her head and smiled.

"No, I just know that you like your coffee."

Star reached for her telephone and began dialling.

"Maybe later," Star said as she placed the receiver by her ear.

Sally smiled and left the office.

"Hello, forensics?" Star said.

"Yes?"

"It's DS Star Bellamy. I have the warrant to search Camden White's BMW motor vehicle. Do you have your team on standby?"

"We're packed up and ready to leave when you are."

"Great job, thank you," Star said. "I'll call you when we're ready to move."

Star hung up and brought Detective Inspector Pratt up to date with a text message. She received her reply immediately: 'Keep me posted. DI Pratt.'

***

Star, Sally and the forensic team waited out of sight at the end of the road where Camden White lived in Clapham. His BMW was parked on the driveway. Star watched as Robin and two uniformed police officers escorted him down the pathway and then into the waiting police car. As the car disappeared out of sight, Star gave the signal for the forensics team to move forward. The cars raced down the road and came to a stop directly outside the house. The senior forensics officer had a tape perimeter set up around the suspect's motor vehicle. Star had watched the team at work on a number of occasions and was impressed by how diligently they adhered to the standard operating procedures. They understood that the modern criminal justice system was challenging and that the principles and practices of the forensic investigation had to be watertight for a legally defensible process. Star watched as the team unlocked the car with ease. The forensic team wore their standard issue Tyvek suits. The full white body suit with hood, mask, booties and gloves are all made from a highly dense polyethylene and worn over their clothes to avoid contamination. Star and Sally looked on intently as the forensic team scoured every millimetre of the car. The lead forensic officer gave instructions for Luminol to be brought from the car. Star understood that Luminol is a chemical that gives off chemiluminescense, a blue glow, and is used to detect signs of blood after a stain has been cleaned. Three hours later the lead forensic officer ordered the team to finish up and then approached Star.

"How did you get on?" Star asked.

"We found six hairs and some fibre samples. The Luminol test has produced signs of blood, so we have something to work with. I can say with certainty that the car has been subjected to a thorough clean but there is always something if you look hard enough," said the forensics officer.

"Thank you, great job," Star said with a warm smile.

"We'll get what we have back to the lab and keep you informed."

Star and Sally got back into her Range Rover and drove back across London to the station. She asked Sally to text Robin and ask him to confirm that Camden White was still at the station. He was.

Sally suggested a cup of coffee in the canteen before going down to the interview rooms to see Camden White.

"Do you think we'll get him Sergeant?" Sally said with a glint in her eye.

"If Camden White is guilty then we will get him, Sally," Star said confidently.

"It amazes me, Sergeant, how you always remain so positive. I don't mean to speak out of turn here but, in my view, DI Pratt is riding on the tails of the good work you do and yet you still just get straight on to the next case," Sally said in a lowered voice.

"DI Pratt is a senior officer and therefore my role is not to question him, and I would strongly suggest that where he is concerned you keep your views and thoughts to yourself. You're a good police officer, Sally, and with time you will go far," Star said as she leant back in the chair.

"Sorry Sergeant. I didn't mean any disrespect and I will keep my views to myself," Sally said as she lowered her head.

"Don't give it another thought," Star said with a reassuring smile.

"I do worry, well not exactly worry, but I have been a little concerned by recent events," said Sally.

"What exactly is on your mind?"

"A few of us have been reading through the recent national statistics and it's a concern that nine out of ten crimes are not being properly reported. I can't understand what the force as a whole has to gain by under-reporting crimes. Surely the public will lose faith in us to police the streets on their behalf if they think we're not capable or don't have the resources to tackle the real challenges," said Sally.

"I've read the same report and the headlines are a little misleading," said Star.

"It reads that the Derbyshire force failed to record over thirty thousand crimes," Sally said bluntly.

"Exactly, it can be misleading. Yes, Derbyshire's record has been atrocious but if you follow the stats you'll see that it improves significantly with London at 8% and Kent, Essex and Sussex at just 4%. I'm not justifying anything but the Chief Constables responsible for that key performance indicator will either create a strategy to improve or find themselves replaced. The stats are out in the public domain so there is nowhere to hide," said Star.

"Do you think that as a force we are just vastly under resourced?"

"It may be that senior officers are putting all their resources into solving crimes rather than counting them. The stats show what the problems are and it's up to those officers to make the improvements. If it's resources they need, they should flag it up and say that with a force of x we can only detect and resolve y. However, with more resources we can achieve z. Does that make sense?" Star said as she reached for her coffee.

"Yes, Sergeant it does. Thank you. It's just that reading stats like that can demotivate an officer and have a person question what they're actually doing. I suppose we all need clear objectives and understand what the deliverables are with the available resources," said Sally.

"That was extremely well put, what degree did you take?"

"I did Business Management at Southampton University."

"Oh wow, same as me. What a coincidence. What made you join the force?"

"I witnessed an altercation outside a nightclub that was getting nasty. The police arrived and whilst most of the onlookers stepped back and did what they were told, there was one young man who had clearly had too much to drink and was actively looking for trouble. He threw a punch at the uniformed police officer, and she took him down. He was on the pavement and handcuffed in seconds. I was so impressed at how a woman of my size and stature had managed a volatile situation. She made a difference, and I decided that was what I wanted to do. Make a difference," said Sally. "I'd be lying if I said that my parents were happy about my decision. My father was dead keen for me to come into the family business, but the textile industry held no interest for me. I don't think my mother has ever forgiven me. I think she believed that with me going into the business my father would work fewer hours and eventually retire but you have to do what's right for you, don't you?"

Star nodded in agreement.

"What about you Sergeant?"

"It's a similar story, Sally and driven, like you, by that need to make a difference which is why I'm now going to see our Mr Camden White.

Star finished her coffee, left the canteen and walked down to the interview rooms. She knocked and entered the room where DC Carpenter had been interviewing.

Camden White looked up at Star and began to smile.

"I wondered where you were," Camden said as he lounged back in the chair.

"Okay DC Carpenter, I'll take it from here," Star said as she motioned Robin to leave.

"This was a bit of waste of everyone's time, don't you think?" said Camden. "I've told you everything I know and I'm really not sure what else you expect to hear."

"You should know," Star said as she sat down on the chair opposite Camden, "that we obtained a warrant to search and carry out forensic tests on your car."

Star could see the immediate change in Camden's body language. However, within a few seconds he relaxed again and looked straight into Star's eyes.

"So, what do you hope to achieve from that? Lady Devine and I were lovers, and she has been in my car many times. In fact, we've been intimate in the car as well, so maybe what you'll find traces of could be a little embarrassing," Camden said as he straightened up in the chair.

"We had a full forensics team go over every inch of your vehicle, Camden, and we have found potential evidence worthy of further investigation. But before we do all that, is there anything you feel you need to share with us? This is your opportunity to share something that you haven't before," Star said as she returned Camden's intense stare.

Camden paused for a few seconds.

"On second thoughts you might not find traces of anything embarrassing because I had the car thoroughly valeted last week. So no, nothing to share that I haven't already told you," said Camden.

"Okay," Star said as she stood up. "You are free to leave Mr White."

"Good, I have an appointment with one of my regulars in an hour," Camden said with a wry smile while looking down at his watch.

Star opened the interview room door and allowed Camden to leave first. She followed him down the short hallway towards the Custody Sergeant's office. She felt as though she had just hit a wall of frozen air. As she looked up, she saw the apparition of Lady Devine. She was pointing intently towards Camden White. A loud, high pitched shrill scream assaulted her ears. She immediately dropped her folder and placed her hands over ears. Camden did the same.

"What the hell was that?" Camden yelled.

The hallway lights began to flicker on and off and then a mountain of paperwork flew off the Custody Sergeant's desk and down the hallway. Several folders smashed into Camden's body and fell to the floor while three interview room doors slammed shut.

The high-pitched shrill scream stopped, the lights stopped flickering, and the temperature began to slowly rise. Star looked over to where the apparition of Lady Devine had been. She had gone.

"You people want to get this placed sorted out," Camden said as he stepped gingerly over the files and paperwork. "One minute you're freezing your nuts off and the next it's all back to normal. This place is strange, very strange."

"You might have to get used to this," thought Star. *"Lady Devine wants justice for what you've done, and I will get it for her. You, Camden White, are an evil, callous, murderer and I will take you down."*

***

Star left the office early and headed for her home in Kensington. She had packed up several folders which she planned to read through that evening. As she walked down the corridor, she had an overwhelming feeling that she should call in on her friend and neighbour, Maude. She rang the bell and waited several seconds before ringing it a second time. The door swung open and Tracey North, the cleaner, stood in the opening.

"Good evening, Tracey, is Maude at home?" Star said with a friendly smile.

"No!"

"Okay, do you know when she'll be home?"

"She's been taken into hospital," Tracey said bluntly.

"Oh no, what's wrong with her?" Star said putting her hand on her heart.

"How would I know, she's old! What do you expect?" Tracey said as she stepped back and slammed the door shut.

Star was stunned.

"What hospital Tracey?" Star called out as she knocked on the door again.

There was no answer. Star battered the door several more times.

"I said, what hospital is she at?" Star yelled through the closed door.

"I don't know. Probably one of those private ones you rich people use," Tracey called back.

"I dislike that woman more than I've ever disliked anyone in my life," thought Star. *"She's a horrible, ignorant, and thoroughly rude individual who should have been sacked years ago."*

Star stepped back, rubbed her sore hands and shook her head in disbelief. She turned to her door, placed her key in the lock and let herself in.

"I hope Maude is alright. I'll need to try and find out where she is. I don't know what's wrong with her, it could be a nasty fall, an existing ailment or maybe, God forbid, a heart attack. With private medical care I'm not sure where to even start looking. I'll find some time tomorrow and try to track her down," thought Star.

Chapter 17

Star had arranged for a team meeting with Detective Constables Robin Carpenter and Sally York. Detective Inspector Ronald Pratt was invited to join them. However, he declined, as he had a pre-arranged meeting but asked for a summary to be emailed to him.

"Robin, have you spoken with forensics?" Star said as she cupped her coffee mug.

"I have Sergeant," Robin said as he rifled through his notes.

"Do you want the long version, Sergeant?"

"I can read through the report later, but for now I just want the conclusion," Star said as she placed the mug on her desk.

"Forensics tested everything they had gathered from Camden White's car boot and confirmed that the fibres were from Brandon Fenton's clothing," Robin said as he placed the document he'd just read from on Star's desk.

"What about the blood?" Star said as she began to rub her chin and listened intently.

"Forensics said that it was just too deteriorated for analysis. I asked them to double check Sergeant. It didn't go down too well, but they did it anyway," Robin said as he shook his head. "It was too deteriorated."

"Okay, so what we have is incriminating but still circumstantial at best. We need hard evidence to make this case. Camden White is going to walk if we cannot place Brandon Fenton in the boot of that car," Star said firmly. "Do we have anything else?"

Robin placed the second sheet on Star's desk and then quickly scanned over the third.

"Hairs taken from Brandon Fenton during the post-mortem, and those that were found in the car were just too damaged to make a conclusive analysis," said Robin.

Star sighed and shook her head slowly.

"The reports says that forensics couldn't analyse the hair's root structure as it had been removed by brute force. They could only make a general comparison."

Star began to smile.

"Okay, we're getting close but just not close enough," Star said as she reached for her coffee mug. "Sally, could you contact Gillian Watts, the handwriting expert. Maybe, just maybe, we can find something there."

"Yes, Sergeant." Sally said as she made notes.

"Okay, that's it," Star said as she stood up.

As Robin and Sally were leaving Star called Sally back.

"Yes, Sergeant?" Sally said as she held her pen eagerly to take down instructions.

"Take a seat Sally."

Sally looked a little confused but sat down in the chair directly opposite Star's.

"Are you comfortable talking off the record?" Star said as she sat down.

Sally nodded.

"I heard a rumour that a certain individual has behaved in an unprofessional and inappropriate manner towards you," said Star.

Sally looked a little shocked and uncomfortable.

"I don't want any trouble, Sergeant," muttered Sally.

"Sally, any form of discrimination that includes uninvited comments, inappropriate conduct or behaviour regarding sex, gender or sexual orientation in the workplace is considered sexual harassment," said Star.

Sally paused for a few moments.

"It's like I said, Sergeant, I don't want any trouble," Sally said as she crossed her arms across her chest.

"It doesn't matter who commits the offence, Sally. It could be an outside contractor, a sergeant, an inspector, or even a chief superintendent. If a person's conduct or behaviour creates an uncomfortable environment which makes it difficult to work or interrupts an employee's success, then it is considered unlawful harassment."

"Is this off the record?"

Star nodded and placed her pen firmly on the desk.

"Okay, there was one individual here who made sexual comments about my appearance."

"Was there anything else?"

Sally paused for a few moments and then took a deep breath.

"There was, on one occasion, some inappropriate touching. I felt this person brush up against me and, well, he was clearly excited Sergeant," said Sally.

Star took a deep intake of breath and slowly shook her head.

"It wasn't Robin, was it?"

"Absolutely not, Sergeant, I would have slapped him silly. No, Robin is harmless. He's one of the nice guys."

"I know and you know it's Detective Inspector Ronald Pratt, Sally," thought Star. *"Just say his name."*

"Are you prepared to say who was responsible, Sally?"

"No, Sergeant. What I will say is that once I built up the confidence I confronted the person and told him that should something like that ever happen again, I would report him for sexual harassment. Equally I said that if I believed that my career in the force was being tampered with because of our conversation, I would report the incident to human resources and seek the advice of a solicitor," said Sally.

"What did he say?"

"He apologised, Sergeant, and said it was a misunderstanding," hissed Sally.

"I'm sorry this has happened," said Star.

Sally slowly allowed her arms to drop back to her sides.

"I've dealt with it, Sergeant and now I just want to get back to doing the job that I love," Sally said firmly.

"Okay, but if you need me, Sally, I'll be there.

Sally left the office just as Star's phone beeped. She had a text message.

'Hi Star, its Julia, how are you? xx'

Star began to write up her notes from the meeting for DI Pratt when her phone beeped again.

"I over-reacted Star. I'm sorry. Can we start again? xxx'

Star read the message and placed the phone back on her desk.

"I'm not sure what to do here. Julia is a lovely girl, but I think she may just be a little too demanding on my time right now," thought Star.

Star opened her private email account and saw she had an email from her friends, Jessica and Michael, in Brighton. She opened the message:

Hi Star

I hope that you're well, happy and life in the police force is still exciting. Michael and I have just sold the last property refurbishing project in North Laines and we wanted to pay you the return on your investment. North Laines was one of Brighton's former slums but now it's the cultural and bohemian centre and the gem of East Sussex. We feel incredibly proud and have made a bundle of cash too. Rather than just make the bank transfer we thought you might like to visit us tomorrow evening, maybe even stay over for the weekend like old times.
Lots of Love
Jessica & Michael xxx

Star beamed as she developed a warm, glowing feeling inside as she read through her friend's message. She answered Jessica straight away:

Hi Jessica and Michael

It is, as always, wonderful to hear from you. Well done with your property investments! You must feel very proud of yourselves. I can still remember how passionate and excited about transforming the properties in North Laines you guys were. I would love... love .... love to see you tomorrow night. However, I'm not able to stay over as I have work commitments.

See you tomorrow.

Love

Star xxx

Almost immediately Star's email provider showed a reply:

Hi Star

Can't wait to see you!

Jessica & Michael xxxx

Star continued to smile as she closed down her private email. She reached for her mobile phone and began to text:

'Hi Julia I think we both know that I'm just not in the best place to commit to a relationship right now. You are strong, beautiful and capable. I truly hope that we can still be friends. Love Star xxx'

Star pressed send and placed her phone on the desk. She finished writing up her notes when she had a reply from Julia.

'Just another of life's painful lessons. I'm not sure you did your best or gave it your all, which, on reflection, probably means you didn't deserve somebody like me. Good luck with your career.'

Chapter 18

Star left London early. It was Friday afternoon, and the traffic was notoriously bad leaving the city and travelling on the M25 motorway. She was excited to see her friends. The trio had all studied Business Management together at Southampton University and had built a strong friendship.

As Star sat in the traffic leading through Croydon, she removed the Phil Collins Greatest hits CD and replaced it with a CD she had created whilst at university. As the Range Rover stopped and started in the thick traffic, *'Tik Tok'* by Kresha began to play. With the windows up and the air conditioning on, she turned up the volume and was instantly taken back to her days at Southampton University and the special times with Jessica and Michael. They had forged a friendship quite early on as they progressed in their classes. During the final year the friendship had found another level. The conversations had moved beyond economics, history and social sciences. It was already clear that Jessica and Michael, who had been in a relationship since senior school, would break into buying properties, add value by extending the living area, install new bathrooms and kitchens and then sell on at healthy profit before doing it all over again. The friends would regularly drink at 'The Stag', a campus pub offering great value food and subsidised drinks. Star remembered how the three of them had become a little tipsy one night before returning to her room.

"I've often wondered why so much importance and pressure was placed on one to lose their virginity and gain sexual experience. What do you think Star?" Jessica said as she sprawled back on Star's armchair with her glass of white wine.

"I don't know. Maybe that's why having sex for the first time is so important for some people," Star said as she poured Michael a large glass of white wine.

"I suppose it's a kind of milestone," Michael said as he chinked glasses with Star.

"True, but there must be a mixed bag of memories," Jessica slurred.

"How do you mean?" said Michael.

"You know, awkward, maybe painful and who knows, probably some funny moments too," Jessica said as she raised her glass to Michael. "I know mine was."

"So what was yours?" Star asked as she sat on the edge of her bed. That's if Michael doesn't mind listening."

"Oh, I don't keep anything from Michael, he's the love of my life, my soul mate," Jessica said raising her glass again.

Michael blew her a drunken kiss.

"I had been going out with this guy at school on and off all year. I think I had all my firsts with him, Kieran McKentney. Kiss, fondled by boobs and a hand job. I even did a sleep over once and when he started trying to take things to another level I just chickened out. The following day he ended things with me. I was heartbroken for about four hours. Then I went away on holiday with my parents to the south of France and it was there that I met Pierre. He was tall, handsome and respectful. I suppose I should admit that he was nineteen and I was just fourteen although, to be fair, I did look a lot older. He invited me out to eat, which we did and I'm not quite sure how it happened so fast, but we ended up having sex in the tent he was staying in. To be honest it was nothing like I thought it would be and I remember thinking that maybe I should have had sex with Kieran. I mean he was the most popular boy in his year. To this day I'm not sure why society puts such a big deal on the whole thing. Just be safe and responsible and that's it," Jessica said as she shrugged her shoulders and spilt a little of her wine.

"Oops, sorry."

"That's alright. I have to clean up in the morning anyway," said Star.

"What about you, Star? What was it like for you the first time?" said Jessica

Star looked first at Jessica and then at Michael.

"Oh, come, it's safe to talk. You're with friends," said Jessica.

"The best of friends," said Michael.

"I was seeing this lovely boy called Glen. He really was sweet. We played around as teenagers do, but when he tried to take things further, I just had to place my hand on his chest and stop him. I explained that I had to work up to it. He was wonderful, understanding, and didn't run for the hills in search of someone else to lose his virginity to. We continued to play around together and then finally, while I was babysitting for a neighbour, I just felt I was ready for it and boy, did I enjoy it!" Star said with a cheeky grin. "What about you Michael?"

"Sure you want to hear it?"

"Oh come on, Michael, it's not like I don't already know," said Jessica. "We tell each other everything and that is why I love him so damn much!"

"Okay. Right, it was during the summer, and I had been seeing this girl for about three months which, when we were at school, was quite a long time. A long-term relationship back then was about a month."

Both Jessica and Star chuckled.

"I had heard, through lads' talk, that this girl, Beth, who was quite developed for a fifteen-year-old, had given hand jobs and even a blow job while going out with some of the lads. So, I decided to ask her out and we spent a lot of time together. After awhile we did become a little more intimate, but rather than run after the hand job, I hung in there to see if she would go all the way. I should point out here, ladies, that I had got pretty much zero action throughout high school," chuckled Michael.

Jessica and Star were still chuckling.

"Anyway, one day she invited me over to her parents' home. They were out at a work function and not expected back until the early hours. Beth opened a bottle of wine and we both drank a glass. She then asked me if I had ever seen a pornographic movie. Of course I said no, because I hadn't. She then disappeared off into her father's home study and returned with a blank DVD case. She had this smile, and you can believe me when I say I was excited. She placed the disc into the DVD player and asked me to sit next to her on the sofa. The movie started and until I saw the size of the actor's private parts I had been really excited, thinking we were going to have sex. Then all I could think about was what would she think when she saw mine. I have to admit to being around average here," Michael said with a grin. "When she put her hand on my leg I just forgot about any worries and just went for it. To be totally honest I may have lasted a little over ten seconds the first time, but Beth insisted on coaxing me for a second go. Which I did for maybe ten minutes. Now if she was measuring my performance like the movies, there would be no awards. We never did it again and she started seeing a guy who had already left school and rode around on a motorcycle. I didn't mind because I had lost my virginity and that was what I really wanted."

"That was remarkably honest of you," Star said as she took a large sip from her wine glass.

"Yeah, he's cute like that," said Jessica.

There were a few moments' silence when Jessica gulped down her glass of wine and spoke.

"Star," said Jessica.

"Yes," answered Star.

"I think you're lovely. Can I kiss you?"

Star looked up to see Jessica looking at her with googly eyes.

Star looked over at Michael. Her heart was beating so fast she thought it would burst out of her chest. Star suspected she might be bi-sexual as she had fantasised about both boys and girls.

"I don't mind if you don't" Michael said with a wry smile.

Star found she was nodding as Jessica rose from the chair and walked gingerly towards the edge of the bed where Star was sitting. She lowered herself down onto her knees. The two girls were just inches apart. Star could smell the scent from her 'Divas' by Emanuel Ungaro perfume. The luxurious aroma of pineapple, bergamot and orange was simply divine. Jessica smiled and gazed deep into Star's eyes before slowly edging forward. She was attracted to Jessica and had thought, at times, that maybe through Jessica's flirty mannerisms, she liked her back. Star felt Jessica's hand cup the side of her face and tip her head to the right just before their lips met. For Star it felt like Christmas morning. The kiss lasted several seconds and then Jessica pulled away returning for one last peck on the lips.

"Hmm, that was every bit as wonderful as I've imagined," sighed Jessica.

"You've thought about kissing me before," Star said.

"A lot more than once," Jessica chuckled.

"Star," said Michael.

"Yes,"

"Would you mind if I kissed you too," Michael said as he put his glass down on the coffee table.

Star immediately turned to face Jessica and saw she was smiling.

"It would only be fair," Jessica whispered.

Star nodded.

Michael walked over to Star and held out his hand. She took it and rose to her feet. Michael's deep blue eyes were burning with desire. He was a tall, strong man with an athletic build. Star liked him a great deal, they were great friends, but she had only ever thought of him as Jessica's partner. Michael put his hands on Star's hips and pulled her firmly towards him. Their lips locked and Michael pushed his tongue into her mouth. She became excited when she felt his manhood press up against her. Star could feel his hands pulling her closer when she suddenly felt an arm around her shoulder and then a second pair of lips kissing at her neck and behind her ear. She was inflamed with desire. She felt as though she were having an out of body experience as ripples of pleasure pulsated through her body. The three friends kissed passionately as they edged themselves onto the bed.

***

Star was through the worst of the traffic and was now travelling along the A23 and heading out towards the M23 motorway to Brighton. *"Sex on Fire' by The Kings of Leon'* pounded through the stereo system.

"How very appropriate," thought Star as she chuckled to herself.

As the road opened up into three lanes, Star put her right foot down firmly on the accelerator. The Range Rover responded and very quickly found itself at the legal speed limit. She had forgotten all about work. She was extremely fond of her friends, Jessica and Michael. They had tremendous chemistry between them and no matter long they were apart, the three friends acted as if it had been just days rather than months. As Star turned into her friends' road *'I Gotta Feeling'* by the Black Eyed Peas began to play. Memories of Jessica, Michael and her dancing wildly to the song in a Southampton nightclub came racing back. Star was happy. She parked the car in their driveway. She noticed they had bought a graphite grey BMW X3M, the new high performance version of the compact SUV. Star had visited a BMW showroom in Park Lane, London when she was considering replacing her three-year-old Range Rover. The 503 horsepower and eight speed automatic gearbox had sounded very tempting. However, she chose to keep the Range Rover for another year and then trade it in against a new model.

The front door swung open.

"Star!" Jessica called out as she skipped down the pathway and threw her arms around her friend.

"Wow, you look great!" Star said as she scanned Jessica's slender, svelte figure.

"I've been getting my bikini body in shape for our winter holidays in Cancun, Mexico," Jessica said as she ran her hands down her slender body and finished with a little wiggle. "Do you like my new hairstyle?"

Star ran her eyes back up to Jessica's raven-black hair infused with copper bronze balayage which curtained her heart shaped face.

"Stunning, simply stunning!" Star said as the two friends hugged for a second time.

"It's so good to see you Star. We've missed you... I've missed you," Jessica said before planting a kiss on her cheek.

"Hello Star."

Star looked over to the door, it was Michael. He had bulked out a little since she last saw him. Before, he had an athletic stature, and now he had developed the physique of a body builder. Michael wore a pair of Gucci jeans, a white open necked long-sleeved shirt and a pair of brown Gucci trainers.

"You've certainly been working out, Michael, you look fabulous," Star said as she took Jessica by the hand and walked towards Michael. He embraced her and kissed her on both cheeks.

"It's great to see you, Star. It has to be, what, twelve months?" Michael said as he stepped back and smiled at the two girls still holding hands.

"It might be a little longer," Star said as she shrugged and smiled awkwardly. "I've just been so busy at work."

The three friends went inside where Michael phoned for a taxi to take them to an Italian restaurant he had booked. The restaurant was in a collection of narrow lanes that was famous for its small shops and restaurants. The area had become known simply as the Lanes.

***

"I can't believe how well you both look," Star said as she sipped from her glass of soda water with lime. "Life in Brighton really suits you guys."

Michael refilled his and Jessica's wine glass from a bottle of Veuve Clicquot La Grande Dame. The white wine had a blend of pinot noir and chardonnay giving it a soft gold colour with a hint of jade. Star watched as her friends both swirled their glasses before taking a sip.

"Look how far we have all come in a relatively short time," Jessica said as she placed her glass on the table. "I can still remember our nights out the Dukes Head in Southampton."

"I never liked that place," said Star.

"Me either," said Jessica.

"It wasn't that bad," Michael said with a chuckle.

"We were not welcome," Jessica said with a grin. "Students were not welcome. It almost felt like you had just stepped into a complete stranger's front room when you entered the pub."

"True," said Michael with a chuckle.

"The landlord, Freddie, I think his name was, would always make some quip or pass a remark about us students," said Jessica. "Here they are, the 'shake 'n' flake' bunch, he would say."

"I remember that," Star said as she shook her head. "Why did we keep going back?"

"I can remember Freddie asking me if I knew what a malapropism was. I'm sure I was on my fifth drink and just shook my head," said Jessica.

"Did he tell you?" Star said as she leant in closer to the table.

"He certainly did. With great delight he informed me that a malapropism is when you confuse a millennial for a regular human being and treat them as a non-stereotypical person," said Jessica. "I've never forgotten that."

"Didn't he initiate some kind of contest by asking each person in the pub to describe a millennial in one word," said Michael.

"You were drunk, Michael, but you're right, he did. The older men in the pub scorned us with 'self-obsessed, entitled, lazy, pampered and not forgetting self-absorbed'. It would make my day if they could see us now. You, Star, a Detective Sergeant in the Metropolitan police and Michael and I with a multi-million-pound property portfolio, all built from our hard work, drive and vision. I would bet money now that they're all still sitting in the same pub nursing their pints of cheap lager and talking about the same stuff," Jessica said triumphantly.

"I wouldn't take that bet," chuckled Star.

"Me either," said Michael.

The friends enjoyed talking about their university days while they relished the three-course meal. Michael ordered a second bottle of wine. Star resisted the temptation of a single glass and continued to sip her soda water with lime.

"Michael has now completed all the accounts and we're thrilled to tell you, Star, that we are able to give you a thirty-three per-cent return on your investment with us. It's more than we initially talked about but with firm negotiation we bought low and sold high." Jessica said with a broad smile.

"That is fantastic, thank you," said Star. "Well done! You must both be very proud of what you've achieved."

"We are, Star, and we couldn't have completed the project without your trust, friendship and investment, so we wanted to show our gratitude," said Jessica.

"So, what's next?" asked Star.

"Well, we have seen several properties which are ripe for restoration and have significant potential for profit," Michael said as he poured himself a healthy measure of wine. "Our thoughts are to try and get the deal done and then take a month or so out in Cancun before coming back and throwing ourselves into it."

"That sounds like a plan," said Star.

"Do you know what we'd really like, Star?" Jessica said as she gazed intently at Star.

"What?"

"For you to come in as a full partner with us," said Jessica.

"I'm more than happy for you to retain my initial investment and the very generous return for your next project," said Star.

"We mean as a full business partner, Star. Jessica and I would love to have you as an everyday part of our business," said Michael.

"And our lives," Jessica said as she reached out and squeezed Star's hand.

"I'm truly flattered. I really am, but I have a career in the police force and I'm good at my job," Star said.

"Would you think about it?" asked Jessica.

"We would both like, very much, to have you as an integral part of both our business and personal lives," said Michael.

"We love, care for and respect you, Star," Jessica said as she squeezed Star's hand tighter.

"I don't know," said Star. "You know how I feel about you both. We have a connection, a chemistry that just works."

"Believe me, Star, Michael and I have talked about this for hours and hours," Jessica said as she lowered her voice. "Everything about our three-way relationship both at university and since has worked because it's fluid. There have been no grey areas between us, and we have clear cut boundaries. That is why it has been so amazing and for us; pretty much perfect. We both love how you've never been afraid to express yourself and know exactly what you want to stay happy with us and the relationship. I am as happy and excited by watching you with Michael as Michael is when he's watching you and I play together. We are all transparent in what we do and what we want and that has been key to us leading up to this conversation. From my own perspective, Star, I understand that I will need to make compromises, there can be no room for insecurity, and I believe that with you that could never happen. We are only here once and we should live freely, without judgement, and just do things that are fun and make us all happy."

"You know that I love you both, with all my heart," said Star. "I wasn't expecting this so please forgive me if I seem a little shocked and hesitant."

"We understand," Michael said with a soft smile. "Neither of us expected you to race back to London, hand in your notice with the police, sell your home in Kensington and then move down and live happily ever after in Brighton with us."

Star nodded in agreement.

"Our special relationship has always been about openness, being honest with ourselves and communication with each other and a willingness to learn. These are strong, positive foundations that could sustain happiness for a lifetime. Will you give it some thought?" Jessica said as she squeezed Star's hand for a final time and then reached for her glass of wine.

"I will but I wouldn't want to be put under time pressure. Equally, it would break my heart if I were to lose my special friendship with you both if what you're proposing just wasn't right for me at this time. You've certainly given me a great deal to think about," said Star.

Michael raised his glass.

"To special friendships and long may they continue."

"Special friendships," Jessica said as she raised her glass.

Star smiled and raised her glass.

Michael and Jessica ordered Rémy Martin brandies and then insisted on paying the full bill. The waiter called them a taxi, which took them back through the busy streets of Brighton and to Michael and Jessica's home. Once inside the house, Michael ground some coffee beans and made coffee. Star could feel the chemistry between them. It was comfortable and as she looked at her watch she thought: *'Oh what the hell, the roads will be clearer in the early hours.'*

Jessica finished her coffee, smiled, and then stood up. Star could feel the electricity in the air as Jessica began to slowly peel off her clothes. She couldn't believe how beautiful Jessica's body looked in her matching royal blue bra and panties. Michael rose from his armchair and unbuttoned his jeans and slowly edged them down over his muscular thighs and down to his feet. He undid his crisp white shirt exposing a muscular, toned, physique. Jessica and Michael were both standing in their underwear. Jessica tossed her hair back and smiled seductively at Star. Both Michael and Jessica held out their hands before leading Star through to their bedroom.

***

Star kissed both Jessica and Michael goodbye before they opened their front door so she could leave for London. They had both pleaded with her to stay the night and go for breakfast in the morning on the seafront. Star wanted to stay but she had work commitments. She started her Range Rover and drove slowly through Brighton, passing several groups on their way home after a late night of clubbing. Once on the M23 motorway she turned on her car stereo and slipped in a random CD. As she relaxed back in the seat, *'Born this Way'* by Lady Gaga began to play.

Star smiled as the song allowed her mind to wander back to her younger days when she had attended London pride, the Mardi Gras of all parades, at Trafalgar Square with Jessica and Michael. The three friends arrived at Baker Street just before 1.00 pm by underground and were quickly swallowed up by a sea of ruby red costumes and happy, excited, people. Thousands from the gay community, from all over London, had come together to celebrate all things LGBT. The parade had extra importance as it celebrated the 40th year of the Gay Liberation Front's Annual festival. The three friends joined thousands of like-minded people as they marched down Oxford Street and Regent Street and finally joined everyone partying at Trafalgar Square. Star remembered how she felt as she watched and listened to the live music, stage performers and spontaneous dancers. She smiled to herself as remembered how Jessica, Michael and she had all blown their whistles and laughed until their cheeks ached.

"I never expected Jessica and Michael to suggest that we all live and work together," thought Star. *"I can see why it would work, not just for them, but for me too. We have a connection, a chemistry that is rare and may only come along once in a lifetime."*

Star sighed.

"It would be great to share a life with my closest friends and I just know that there would never be any issues. Our love is true and runs deep," thought Star. *"But I'm not sure I would be content buying, renovating and then selling on properties. I don't need the money and I just can't imagine that being as satisfying as tracking down and bringing a killer to justice. That is what I am meant to be doing. This is the path I was meant to take."*

The Lady Gaga track came to an end and *'Vogue'* by Madonna began to play. Star reached out and turned up the volume.

"What about the visits I have from the dead asking for help?" thought Star. *"I have never shared that secret with either Jessica or Michael.*

No, that part of my life is to remain private, but I just don't know how I could manage that without having my own place, but then that just defeats the point of us sharing an all-encompassing life together. Could I take the plunge and just share it, or would that frighten them off? I couldn't bear not to have them in my life or to somehow tarnish our friendship. No, it has to stay private."

Star began to slowly shake her head.

"No, I'll have to decline, but not straight away. I want them but I also want my life in the force. What you're telling yourself, Star, is that you want your cake, and you want to eat it. Something us bi-sexuals get accused of all the time. Jessica and Michael will understand," thought Star.

The Madonna track was replaced by *'True Colours'* by Cyndi Lauper.

"How very appropriate this track is," thought Star. *"I still don't know where my life as a medium and psychic will take me. Mother told me over and over that one day I would be called upon just as she was, but she never said any more no matter how hard I pushed for answers. I miss you mum, and I miss our chats."*

'Honey' by Kehlani began to pound through the speakers. Star immediately turned down the volume and then as she settled back into her seat, she found herself thinking about Shirley Fenton.

"There is something very charismatic, sexy and charming about you Mrs Fenton," thought Star. *"You're almost like that character 'Catwoman' from that old Batman television show from the 1960's, only you really are the Queen of the bad guys."*

Star found herself smiling as she replayed conversations with Shirley Fenton and her body language.

"I think maybe she was coming on to me. Letting me know she knew that I am attracted to women. Or was she? I shouldn't even be thinking

like this. I have a job to do and daydreaming about what intimacy would be like with Shirley Fenton, nice as those thoughts are, just isn't right!" thought Star.

It was 3.00 am when Star looked in her rear-view mirror and saw the police car's lights flashing behind her. She looked down at her speedo. It read 74 mph. Star understood that the police guidance in relation to speeding offences was the officer had discretion when the speeding vehicle registers the speed limit plus 10% plus another 2 mph. Star's speed was within the officer's discretion. She indicated to pull over onto the hard shoulder and then came to a slow stop. The police car pulled up behind her. She reached into her handbag for her driving licence. The officer got out of the car and swaggered up to the driver's side window. Before Star could press the electric window switch the officer rapped his knuckles on the glass.

"Good evening officer," Star said with a smile.

"Madam I have observed you committing a traffic violation on my in-car camera system. What speed do you think you were travelling at?" said the officer.

"I do apologise, officer, I believe I was doing 74 mph," Star said, looking a little crestfallen.

"You think that it's alright to just ignore the speed limit, do you?"

"No, I certainly don't. It's 3.00 am and there is no traffic on the road and just for a moment I exceeded the speed limit. It was wrong and I can assure that it will not happen again," Star said with a broad smile.

The officer stepped back and looked at the Range Rover.

"Where have you just come from?"

"I've been visiting friends in Brighton," said Star.

"Is this your car?"

"It is," Star said nodding.

"Does your husband know that you're sneaking around Brighton in the dead of night in the car he's probably paying hire purchase payments on? Where is your husband? Working away, is he? What is it, while the cat's away the mouse will play?" the officer said with his tone becoming increasingly aggressive.

"This is my car and I'm not married," Star said assertively. "I have apologised and admitted to the speeding offence."

"So, you think that's enough, do you?"

Star remained quiet.

"I am a representative of the law and you, bitch, are a criminal, a law breaker and you will sit there until I'm done with you. Now, don't think, even for a minute, that fluttering your eyelashes will help your cause here, because you look too much like my skanky ex-wife. Now that was one dirty, underhanded, teaser!"

Star tried to keep her patience but then slammed her hand forcefully down on the steering wheel.

"I understand the pressure on uniformed police officers to consistently deliver road traffic violations but you're becoming very aggressive, unprofessional and you're trying to intimidate me. Your blatant misogynistic behaviour undermines the trust and confidence of local communities and damages the reputation of good, hardworking, police officers," Star said firmly.

"Who the hell do you think you are? See this uniform?" the officer said as he took two steps back and rubbed both hands down his trousers legs. "This uniform means if I tell you to jump then you reply how high, sir!"

"I have admitted my wrongdoing and I pulled over in the vague hope that you would use your discretion to waiver my fixed penalty notice with a warning. What I will not do is sit here and listen to your disgraceful behaviour and still take the fine. You are bordering on gross misconduct and there is no place in the modern police force for people like you!"

The officer was angry, red faced and lost for words.

"If, and I do mean if, I were a member of the public then I would report this incident to the Independent Office for Police Conduct but since I have your badge number and know the force you represent, I will take my complaint directly to the Chief Superintendent," Star said assertively.

"You mean you're a police officer?"

Star reached into her handbag and produced her warrant card.

"Detective Sergeant Star Bellamy. I'm CID with the Met," Star said as she returned her warrant card to her handbag.

The officer's demeanour changed immediately. He feigned a false smile.

"You should have made yourself known earlier. We police have to stick together," the officer said in an awkward tone.

Star started her engine and pressed the electric window button. It slowly rose as Star slid the gear shift into 'Drive', put her indicator on and began to move back onto the M23 motorway. She looked in her rear-view mirror and saw the officer was still standing on the hard shoulder.

"To coin Shirley Fenton's expression, we have yet another dinosaur that needs to be made extinct," thought Star. *"After that sickening,*

diabolical, behaviour you can be sure your days in that uniform are numbered!"

Chapter 19

Star had instructed Detective Constables Robin Carpenter and Sally York to bring Camden White back to the station for further handwriting analysis. On his arrival he was taken through to the interview rooms where Gillian Watts M.BIG (Dip), one of the UK's leading handwriting experts, was making preparations.

"Thank you for coming at such short notice, Mrs Watts," Star said as she shook Gillian's hand.

"My pleasure," Gillian said as she continued to lay out the table.

"Yes, thank you, and then I can be excluded from further investigations and just get on with my life," Camden White said as he sat at the table. "Polygraph tests, long, pointless, interviews when you should be out there doing your job."

"I appreciate you helping us eliminate you from further enquiries, Mr White," Star said without looking in his direction.

"Good, because I have an appointment with a regular client later, so please just get on with it," Camden said as he slouched back in the chair.

The science of handwriting analysis is based on the assumption that no two individuals can create exactly the same handwriting and that an individual cannot reproduce his own handwriting, otherwise known as variations. Variations are natural deviations that occur in a person's handwriting.

"Gillian, I'll be in my office if you need me," Star said as she left the interview room.

"You are guilty as sin, Camden White!" thought Star.

∗ ∗ ∗

Star returned to her office with a fresh mug of coffee just in time to take to take a phone call.

"Hello, is that Detective Sergeant Star Bellamy?" said a man's voice.

"It is," Star replied, "How can I help you?"

"I'm Miles, Miles Travistock," he said, "We have met, albeit some time ago when I was visiting my aunt, Maude.

"Yes, I do remember you. How are you and how is Maude?"

"Perplexed, and more than a little bit concerned for the safety of my aunt," Miles replied.

"Why?" Star asked.

Miles said, "I've just been in to see my aunt and I read through the doctor's report. It shows that she had traces of Diazepam in her blood. Now I know for an absolute fact that Diazepam is not one of the medications my aunt takes.

"Have you spoke to Maude about it? Star asked.

"The fall from her dizzy spell has left her fragile and she's struggling to remember key things," Miles said. "I'm not sure if you know this, Star, but Diazepam has a huge number of side effects that includes memory loss after a certain event."

"What are trying to say?"

"I believe that my aunt was given this drug by a third party."

"Who do you believe would purposely give Maude a potentially life-threatening drug?" Star said.

"The cleaner, Tracey!" Miles replied vehemently.

Star said "That is a pretty strong allegation. Do you have any proof?"

"I'll be honest with you Star," Miles said, "I've never liked or trusted her. She's rude and I've caught her rolling her eyes when my aunt talks to me about her conspiracy theories."

"Your aunt's cleaner is an acquired taste, and she certainly has the trust of your aunt," Star said

"Yes, she does, and she has access to all kinds of personal information," Miles said. When the doctor pointed out the traces of Diazepam, I decided to delve a little deeper. Now, as her eldest nephew, my aunt gave me the passwords to her personal banking account amongst other important information. When I checked last night, I discovered that £175,000 has been transferred to the cleaner's personal account."

"Do you have evidence?" Star asked.

"Yes," Miles said, "I've printed off the statement. I am deeply concerned, Star, that my aunt is being drugged and robbed.

"Have you spoken to either Maude or Tracey about it?"

"No. I was going to, but with the Diazepam in my aunt's blood and with theft being a criminal offence, I thought it was best to call you," Miles said

"You did the right thing," Star said reassuringly

"Thank you," Miles replied.

"Please message me the hospital and ward Maude is in, Miles, and we'll both go and visit her. Make sure you bring the printed bank statement with you. Remember, not a word to anyone, are we clear?"

"Yes, and thank you, Star. I've not slept and have been truly troubled over this."

Star ended the phone call.

Star knew Diazepam to be a potentially lethal prescription drug if taken in large doses. It's commonly used to treat a range of medical conditions that include anxiety, seizures and alcohol withdrawal. Star was concerned. When Miles messaged the whereabouts of his aunt, she made arrangements to meet him there at 6.00 pm.

Two hours later there was a knock at Star's office door. It was Gillian Watts, the handwriting expert.

"Hi Gillian, come in," Star said as she beckoned her over to her desk. "Would you like some tea or coffee?"

"No, no thank you," Gillian said as she placed her files on Star's desk.

"As you probably know, Detective Sergeant Bellamy, handwriting involves a comparative analysis and I've examined both the ransom note you made available and the test subject, Mr Camden White's handwriting. I have analysed for distinctive characteristics that include letters, word spacing, letter and word slant, size and the proportionality of letters, unusual formations of letters, flourishes and other individual attributes." Gillian said as she pulled her reading glasses from their resting position on her forehead.

"Okay," Star said as leant forward over the desk.

"The next thing I did was differentiate elements from both documents. I looked at the spelling, grammar, punctuation and phraseology," Gillian said, looking up briefly from reading her document.

"And then?" quizzed Star

"I evaluated all the similarities. The differences are a good indication of a non-match, no single similar characteristic; no matter how unique can fully determine a match. Therefore, all likenesses must be considered."

"Have you come to a conclusion?" Star asked.

Gillian looked up from her paperwork and put the document on the desk.

"Oh yes, Detective Sergeant Bellamy, I have."

Star motioned Gillian to continue.

"Following my extensive analysis of the unique characteristics in the handwriting of both documents I have concluded that Mr Camden White did indeed write the ransom letter," Gillian said with a brief smile.

"Yes!" thought Star.

"That is excellent news, thank you, Gillian," Star said, as she struggled to contain her excitement at gaining conclusive, hard, evidence of Camden White's guilt.

Star shook hands with Gillian and then immediately called Detective Inspector Pratt on his mobile phone. It rang several times before going to voicemail. Star opted not to leave a voice message and messaged her senior officer.

'We have conclusive evidence from a leading handwriting expert that Camden White is guilty of Brandon Fenton's murder. DS Star Bellamy.'

Star called the custody sergeant and had Camden White brought back to the interview room. She left her mobile phone on the desk and walked confidently down to the interview rooms. As she entered the room, she saw Camden look at his watch before slouching back in the chair.

"Well, is that it?" Camden said, as he put both hands behind his head

"Yes, that is it," said Star.

"Well, can I go now?" Camden said, as he leant forward and looked down at his watch again.

"No, you can't," Star said firmly. "Mr Camden White I am formally arresting you for the kidnap and murder of Mr Brandon Fenton. You do not have to say anything, but it may harm your defence if you do not mention when questioned something which you later rely on in court. Anything you do say will be given in evidence."

"No, no, no! You can't arrest me, I'm innocent! I did not murder Lady Devine; she was my friend, my lover. You've made a terrible mistake!" Camden yelled.

Star opened the interview door and called in the custody sergeant in.

"This is bloody mad, all wrong! I demand to be let free now!" Camden screamed.

"Mr White we will require you to make a statement," Star said calmly.

"I want a solicitor. I know my rights!" Camden said as he jumped to his feet.

The custody sergeant stepped forward. Camden held his hands up in a submissive gesture.

"The custody sergeant will take you back to the police cells and then call a solicitor for you," Star said as she motioned for the custody sergeant to remove him from the interview room.

"Gotcha!" Star hissed under her breath while punching the air once the interview room was clear.

Star returned to her office and found a text message had been left from DI Pratt.

'Good, I'll be in first thing in the morning for a complete update. DI Pratt.'

Star read it and then put the phone back on the desk.

"Not even a well done, good job, nothing. But I bet he'll be spinning some yarn to those upstairs about how he co-ordinated the investigation," thought Star. *"It makes me sick to my stomach when somebody else gets the credit for another person's good police work. Pratt has probably been doing it since day one!"*

***

After Maude collapsed at her home in Kensington, she was taken by ambulance to the Chelsea & Westminster NHS hospital. It has four hundred and thirty beds and is located in Chelsea. Star paid and parked in the car park and met Miles in the hospital reception at 6.00 pm as planned.

"Detective Sergeant Bellamy?" Miles said as he reached out his hand.

Miles had a bronzed complexion and was six foot tall in his dark blue suit. He had a slim waist and short brown hair styled into the popular white collar workers side parting. His eyebrows were pencil thin, crowning his big walnut brown eyes.

"Yes, but please, call me Star. Your Aunt Maude is more than just my neighbour, she's my friend," Star said as she shook his hand. "Can I see the bank statements?"

"Sure," Miles said as he handed her three printed sheets.

Star scanned her eyes over them to where Miles had highlighted the first suspicious transfer of £25,000, then on page two was a transfer of £50,000, and on the final page was a transfer of £100,000.

"Miles, are you sure your aunt never mentioned making a loan or giving a gift to Tracey?" Star said as she folded the paperwork and placed it in her handbag.

"Definitely not!"

"Okay. Let's go up and see Maude and please leave the key questioning to me, okay?"

Miles nodded.

"Yes, sure. Whatever you say, Star."

Star and Miles took elevator 'C' up to the Chelsea Wing for private inpatients on the fourth floor. Maude, as a private inpatient, had access to the hospital's specialist facilities, consultants, and expert care and was staying in a private hotel style room with en-suite. Star and Miles stood by the door to her room and looked in.

"Remember, Miles, I ask the questions," Star whispered.

They entered the room. Maude was sitting up, but had her eyes closed.

"Hello Maude, are you awake?" Star said quietly.

Maude's eyes popped open.

"Hello Star, how nice of you to visit," Maude said in a low croaky voice.

"Hello, aunt," said Miles.

"Well, if it isn't my favourite nephew, Miles," Maude said with a warm smile.

Star, Miles and Maude talked about the circumstances that led up to her fall.

"How was Tracey when you became dizzy?" Star said as she sat on the corner of Maude's bed.

"It's all very fuzzy," said Maude.

"That would be the effects of the Diazepam, Maude. When did you start taking those?" Star said as she reached out and squeezed Maude's hand.

"I've never taken Diazepam in my life," Maude said adamantly.

"Are you absolutely sure?" Star said as she raised her right eyebrow.

"Yes," said Maude.

"Was it Tracey who called the ambulance?"

"I think so. All I can remember is falling and then looking up and Tracey was standing over me with her hands on her hips. She seemed to be just standing there looking down at me for ages and the next thing I knew I was in an ambulance and then here," said Maude.

"How have you and Tracey been getting along recently?" said Star.

"Actually, she has been almost like a changed person. I think I told you that when we had tea at Claridges," said Maude. "She's even been bringing me the most delicious Eton Mess as a treat.

"You did. Maude, have you made a loan or gifted any money to Tracey recently?" Star said as she let go of Maude's hand and slipped her hand into her handbag.

"Money? I don't understand?" said Maude.

"Have you lent Tracey a sum of money or perhaps made a gift of it?" said Star.

"No, very definitely not," said Maude.

"Do you know what these are?" Star said as she opened the printed copies of her bank statement.

Maude looked at the first page and then scanned her eyes over all three pages.

"That's my bank statement, but they've made some kind of mistake," Maude said as she forced herself to sit up.

"What isn't right about it, Maude?" Star said as she poured her a glass of orange squash.

"I never made those transfers. It must be some kind of banking error," said Maude.

"Did you see who the recipient was?"

"Yes, Tracey. That's why it must be some kind of a mistake. I would never loan or give away £175,000 to my cleaner. That is preposterous," said Maude indignantly.

Star could see that she was confused and getting agitated.

"If you did not loan or gift that money to Tracey and the bank confirms that the transfer was made, what do you think has happened?" said Star.

"Tracey may be a lot of things but she's not a thief," said Maude.

"Maude, how long have you been having those dizzy spells and then passing out?"

"They started about a month ago," said Maude.

"Was Tracey with you when they happened?" Star said as she placed the printed bank statement back into her handbag.

"Yes, I think so. Tracey always makes my afternoon Earl Grey at the same time every day. She then gave me my 'Eton Mess' treat. It is then that I just start to feel a bit dizzy. It must be my age or something."

"Okay Maude. I believe that we may have a situation here so I'm going to have one of my officers come and visit you here and take a statement. Can you do that for me?" Star said as she reached over and squeezed Maude's hand.

"Do you think Tracey has stolen my money, Star?" Maude said sadly.

"I'm going to speak with Tracey to see if we can shed some light on the situation," Star said as she edged off the bed.

Star looked down at her watch. Having charged Camden White with the murder of Brandon Fenton she had to visit Shirley Fenton and give her the news.

***

Star had called ahead to DC Sally York to meet her in Cheyne Walk. She understood that the death of Shirley Fenton's son, Brandon, would be an emotional and stressful time. Star parked the Range Rover behind the Fenton's Bentley. Star quickly scanned the area but couldn't see the chauffeur. Sally locked her car door and quickly joined Star as she walked towards the front door.

"No matter how many times you do these, it never gets easier," whispered Sally.

"I'd start questioning myself if it did," Star said, as she reached up to press the doorbell.

The door opened and they were met by Buster and ushered in. They both followed Buster down the hallway. When they entered the room, they found Mrs Shirley Fenton with her sons Reece and Connor.

"You must be Detective Sergeant Star Bellamy," said the youngest of the men. "I'm Connor."

Star shook his hand.

"I'm Reece."

"Perhaps you might all like to make yourselves comfortable," said Star.

Star could feel the intensity of the family's stare before she finished her sentence. Instinctively Shirley closed her eyes, shook her head slowly and turned away. Reece and Connor remained standing.

"Earlier today, having obtained conclusive evidence, we arrested Mr Camden White for the kidnap and murder of your son, Brandon," Star announced.

"Camden White! He's fucking dead! There isn't a cave on the planet for him to hide in," Reece yelled as he thumped his hand on the desk.

"Reece," Shirley said calmly, "We don't share our thoughts with anyone but the family."

"I'm just upset mum," Reece said lowering his voice. "Please accept my apologies for the emotional outburst."

"That is completely understandable," Star said in her best comforting voice.

"Has the post-mortem been completed?" said Connor.

"Yes," Star answered softly.

"I don't mean to sound matter of fact, but what are the next steps? I've never lost a brother before," said Connor.

"We have some of Brandon's personal items which I'll arrange to have returned to you. You will need to get a medical certificate from the coroner so you can register your brother's death. You will need to do this within five days. The documents you'll need for the funeral will follow shortly after," said Star. "Connor, you will need your brothers National Insurance Number, NHS number, and date and place of birth."

"Okay, I can do that," said Connor.

Star reached into her handbag and then handed Connor a Met Bereavement Advice booklet.

"The death of a loved one can be a deeply traumatic event and will affect people in different ways. The emotions attached to grieving can become, for some, overwhelming. You will find contact details for the Citizens Advice Bureau, Samaritans and Cruse Bereavement Care."

"Thank you, Sergeant," said Connor.

"Yes, thank you," said Reece.

"I understand this is a difficult time for you, Mrs Fenton, but please do not hesitate to contact me if you need my assistance," Star said as she looked on at Mrs Shirley Fenton holding herself and the family together with grace and dignity.

"Thank you, Star," Shirley said as she stood upright and pushed her shoulders back.

"I'll show you out," said Connor.

Chapter 20

Star turned over and reached for the glass of water that she usually placed on her bedside cabinet every night. When she couldn't find it, she turned the bedside lamp on. Although it was a small light it was enough to illuminate the entire bedroom. Star sighed tiredly, got out of bed and walked down the hallway where she turned the light on before going into the kitchen. She reached into the cupboard for a glass and took a bottle of still spring water from the fridge. She poured a glass and took a small sip before returning the bottle to the fridge. Star sensed the temperature dropping in the room. At first she thought it was another lost soul looking for help. From the corner of her eye, she spotted a small, black, almost shadowlike object move at great speed across the kitchen doorway. The temperature continued to fall. The rectangular shadow became blurry and then darted back and forth across the doorway. Star could feel a tension growing in her stomach and her chest became tight. She knew this was unlike any visitation she had experienced before. The shadow hovered above the floor for a few seconds and then shot off at a rapid speed down the hallway.

Star's mother had trained her how to use her special gifts and how to protect herself when she didn't want to be contacted by lost spirits. She walked gingerly towards the door and once she was in the hallway, she turned the light on and turned the kitchen light off. It was so cold in the hallway that Star could see her breath in front of her as she cautiously walked back to her bedroom. The hallway lights began to flicker which made Star quicken her pace. As she stepped through her bedroom door, she was met with a hideous rotting sulphur-like stench. Star put the glass of water on the bedside cabinet.

"Hello," said Star. "Whoever you are, I am sorry for any pain or suffering you are experiencing, but this is not a good time."

Star scanned the room for the shadow object.

The room grew colder, and Star found herself rubbing her arms to keep warm. The bedroom lamp flickered several times and Star's eyes were drawn to the far corner of the room. The black shadowy object was there, levitating a metre above the carpet. Star could feel her chest tightening further as the object began to slowly pulsate.

"I am asking you please to respect my privacy and leave my home," Star said, as she positioned both her arms over her chest to protect her herself. The black shadowy object continued to pulsate and was growing. The pungent odour was becoming increasingly overwhelming.

"This is a dark spirit, a negative, low vibration entity," thought Star.

Memories of the training her mother had given her came flooding back. The dark spirits are beings that exist at a lower vibration. Jennifer had told Star about the many planes of energy and each existed vibrating at different levels and on each of these levels different beings existed. Star had listened intently as Jennifer described the lower realms being populated with unethical, selfish amoral beings. They can only exist by attaching themselves to humans like a parasite. They feed off the host's emotions of pain, grief, anger, rage, lust and jealousy.

Star crossed her arms tighter across her aching chest. She knew she must protect herself. The pulsating black entity had grown to twice its size and she could feel its burgeoning evil presence all around her. She closed her eyes and yelled out "Noooo!"

The curtains began to flap around wildly, and the glass of water shot along the dressing table. The glass exploded, scattering fragments of glass and raining water down onto the carpet. The lampshade swung violently back and forth on its cable from the ceiling. Star opened her eyes. The entity had grown to the size of an adolescent while still hovering above the floor. The evil was surrounding her, but she clenched her fists and resisted it with all her might. Her chest was so tight that she was reduced to taking short breaths. The bed sheets began to rise and flap ferociously. Her pillow shot across the bedroom and slammed into her back with such force that it almost knocked her off her feet. Star could feel her physical and psychic energies weakening. Her lungs were full of the rotten odour, and she was now gasping for air.

Suddenly a huge burst of powerful white light lit up the room. Almost immediately Star could feel the entity's grip begin to diminish. The household objects stopped moving. The bed sheets dropped back down onto the bed and the curtains abruptly stopped flapping. The intensity of the light increased so that objects became difficult to see through the powerful blur of light. Star could feel her energies returning. She could breathe freely. She looked at the dark entity as its pulsating decreased. The white energy surrounded the spirit with its overwhelming power. Star heard a horrific scream that vibrated and penetrated her ears.

Everything in the room returned to normal. Star turned to see a clear vision of her mother slowly fade away.

"Mum!" Star yelled out.

"I will return, Star, soon."

The voice and the apparition of Jennifer were gone.

Chapter 21

Star had taken three days of her outstanding holiday and had used that time to analyse her experience of the entity and then the visitation of her mother. It had terrified her that its eerie strength had almost overpowered her. Had it not been for the intervention by Jennifer, she could have had a being attached to her chakra. She had since learnt that these beings will confuse their host and there had been cases where hosts were fooled into believing that they were hearing the voice of a spirit guide and in one case, God. Some victims would become delusional and schizophrenic, while others would suffer with poor physical and mental health. The low-level entities that attach themselves to hosts begin to influence their thoughts, behaviours, perceptions and emotions. They whisper in the host's own mental voice, so they listen and accept it as their own.

It had been difficult for Star to sleep on the first night, as she had gone over and over her experience with the terrifying entity. She became consumed by the message from her mother saying she would return. By the third day Star took a firm grip on her thoughts and decided to park them up and move forward with her life on this realm.

It was 7.00 pm and Star had just put her food bowl into the dish washer along with the cutlery when the apartment's entry buzzer buzzed.

"Who can that be? I'm not expecting anyone," thought Star.

Star pressed the intercom button.

"Hello, can I help you?" said Star.

"Hello Star, Its Shirley, Shirley Fenton. Can I come in?"

"What the hell is she doing here?" thought Star.

"Yes, of course," Star said, and she buzzed her in.

"Alexa," Star called out, "Reduce the volume."

Star had been playing another of her mother's favourite Phil Collins tracks, 'In the Air Tonight.'

She scanned the apartment for anything that looked messy or out of place. It was as she had left it before going food shopping that morning, spotless.

KNOCK!

Star brushed herself down, checked herself in the mirror and opened the door.

"Mrs Fenton. This is a surprise," Star said as she welcomed her into the apartment.

"It's Shirley, Star."

"Of course. Please, come in," Star said as she motioned for Shirley to follow her through to the lounge.

"This is a very nice home you have, Star," said Shirley.

"Thank you. It's not quite Cheyne Walk but it works for me."

"Why is she here?" Star thought.

"You're looking very smart," Shirley said as she sat down and placed a large brown bag on the floor beside the chair. "Have I caught you on your way out? A hot date perhaps?"

Star giggled awkwardly.

"No, no. I've just got in from work and made myself some dinner," said Star.

Star couldn't help noticing that Shirley wasn't wearing her usual matching jacket and skirt power suits. She wore a beige, jersey mini dress with blue trim, gold buttons, a matching belt and matching beige knee length leather boots.

"I like your dress. Is it Gucci?" Star asked as she admired the cut and finish of the garment.

"Yes, it is," Shirley said with a broad smile. "How very nice of you to notice."

"You do look fabulous, Mrs Shirley Fenton, but how do you know where I live and what are you doing here?" thought Star.

"There are times when you have to wear a certain style of clothes to set the tone and to let people know how they can interact with you. My suits tell men that I'm sexy, confident and here to do business and I'm not to be messed with," Shirley said as she gazed at Star.

"So, what does a classy little Gucci number say?" Star said as she admired her dress.

"It says that this is me when I'm not working," Shirley said with a wry smile.

"I'm sorry; would you like a drink, tea or coffee?"

"Do you have anything a little stronger?" beamed Shirley.

"How can you be the head of the most brutal, violent criminal gang in the UK?" thought Star. *"You look and act so… nice."*

"What's your tipple?" Star said as she opened her drinks cabinet.

"I see that you have a bottle of red there?" said Shirley.

"A friend recommended this Wirra Wirra Catapult red wine. It's an Australian Shiraz from the McClaren Vale. I liked it so much that I bought a case," Star said as she chuckled and placed the bottle on the side table and proceeded to remove the cork.

"You're a bit of a wine snob then Star?"

"No, not really but when you find something you like... well, I'm sure you understand," said Star.

"Oh, I do," chuckled Shirley. "Terry, when he was alive, would like to drive through France to a home we have in Monaco. It was always our plan to retire there one day. Anyway, on the way home he would stop off at three Chateaus and load the car up with his favourite wines. I would tell him that we already have more bottles than we could possibly consume before travelling again but he was insistent. Terry wanted his favourite wines so, yes, I do understand, Star."

Star poured the wine into wide bowl burgundy glasses with high sloping sides.

"Ah, a Luigi Bormioli glass. You have exceptionally good taste in glasses too. I have exactly the same set at home. What a coincidence," said Shirley.

"To some it sounds silly, but to me the glass is just as important as the wine," Star said as she handed Shirley the glass.

Star felt Shirley's fingers brush hers. She felt an electrical shock rage through her entire body. She looked up and their eyes met.

"This is a nice surprise, Mrs Fenton, was there something you wanted me to help you with?" Star said in a formal voice.

Shirley took a sip from the glass. She closed her eyes and savoured the wine before answering.

"This is a very nice wine, thank you." Shirley said as she placed the glass on the coffee table.

"Star, I have lost my eldest son. Clearly I'm grieving, but in my line of business you cannot show any weakness, so my pain is real but well concealed. I wanted to thank you for your tenacity and diligence in bringing the guilty party to justice. Under normal circumstances we would manage any attack on my family or our business ourselves. Our reach is far and wide, but this needed a different approach and whilst I'm desperately sad that my son is gone, I am eternally grateful that you have arrested Camden White," Shirley said as she wiped a single tear from her eye.

"You're welcome, I was just doing my job," said Star. "The Crown Prosecution Service has come back with charges of murder, kidnapping, forgery and being in possession of the ransom money. Camden White will do life."

"Good," Shirley said as she repositioned herself so that she faced Star.

Star witnessed how cleverly Shirley compartmentalised the conversation, smiled and started again.

"Anyway, I'm intrigued. Does a pretty girl like you have a boyfriend?" Shirley said in an upbeat voice.

Star shook her head and smiled.

"I can imagine that there have been handsome guys drooling over you from afar, but they are just too afraid to approach you. A 'how's it going' would guarantee that they'd never see you again, so they sit there trying to figure out the best angle," said Shirley.

"Oh, I doubt that," said Star, looking and feeling a little embarrassed.

"I would imagine your fellow officers could be a little intimidated by you and so they're just too scared to come right out and ask you out," said Shirley.

"I've never thought it would be a good idea to be romantically involved with someone I work with," Star said before taking a sip from her glass.

"I can understand that," said Shirley. "Terry has been gone for a while now and there are times when I miss the touch and excitement of being intimate with another person, but it could never be with a person that either works for me or I do business with. The two things, in my view have to be separated."

Star found herself nodding her head.

"I couldn't help but notice how easily you compartmentalise conversations so relationships, yes I can see that too," Star said as she tried to avoid Shirley's eye contact.

"You said romantically involved with someone you work with and not a man that you work with. You don't have to answer me but Star, are you a friend of Dorothy?"

Star nearly choked on her wine. She knew that a woman asking another woman if she was a friend of Dorothy was code for asking if you are gay.

"Are you okay?" Shirley said rising to her feet and instantly began to rub Star's back while she caught her breath.

Shirley rubbed her hands slowly but firmly on her back and then she gently squeezed the back of her neck before returning to her chair.

"It's okay, Star, you don't have to answer that, and I'm sorry if my question shocked or offended you in any way. I know these days everybody can be remarkably open about their sexuality. For me personally, I have always been attracted to both men and women but that was something completely unheard of in my youth.

I had this wonderful friend, Theresa, and we would spend hours chatting, listening to records and when our parents were out, we would kiss passionately and explore each other's bodies. Together we learnt a great deal about what we enjoyed. My first ever climax was with a woman. I suppose, foolishly, I thought Theresa and I would remain together forever but when the men came knocking, we were encouraged, separately, to go out with boys that had good prospects. I would go along and keep things on a superficial level and tell my parents that it just wasn't right, but Theresa had been subjected to far greater peer pressure and so one day she announced she was marrying some Scottish assistant manager of a butcher's shop down the Old Kent Road. I was devastated, Star, because after that we rarely saw each other for any length of time. She would wave and walk on, almost like what we had and what we did amounted to nothing. It was like Theresa had rewritten history," Shirley said before taking a long sip from her glass.

"I'm sorry to hear that, Shirley. That is truly sad," said Star.

"Theresa got engaged, married and moved away to Peckham, and that was the last I saw of her. I did bump into her parents some years later and asked after her. They told me they were grandparents and that Theresa had twins. They were very proud of their son in-law, who was now a fully qualified butcher and was managing his own shop. When they asked me who I had been dating they nearly had a heart attack on the spot when I told them I was seeing Terry Fenton. I watched as the blood ran from their faces. Even back then Terry had a fearsome reputation. I think seeing how they responded made me decide to stay with Terry and even nudge him to pop the question and so that was it. I became Mrs Shirley Fenton."

"It's funny how fate appears to open paths for us," said Star.

"You seem almost vulnerable, Mrs Fenton," thought Star. *"You're both interesting and very attractive. This could get scary."*

"It is, Star. The day I met with Theresa's parents, and then me deciding on settling with Terry changed my life forever. Fate is an extremely powerful force. It can draw the most unlikely people together," Shirley said with her eyes fixed firmly on Star.

"She is hitting on me big time," thought Star.

"I only ever cheated on Terry once and it wasn't with another man. I would never do that because he would have had us both killed. There was a club in Soho that we would drink at occasionally. I was still in my early twenties and can remember catching the eye of a cocktail waitress called Sian. She had escaped from her abusive husband in Wales to the bright lights of London. She was a stunning woman, Star, and had a cute, slender, curvaceous figure in her little waitress outfit. I found myself watching her in her stockings and heels as she served drinks and interacted with the customers. I looked on as men tried to chat her up, but she kept them all at arm's length with a firm, friendly, smile. Sian, with her long midnight black hair swooping down over her shoulders was magnificent. How I wanted to hold her in my arms. My imagination was working overtime. She knew I was attracted to her. She would catch me admiring her curves out of the corner of her eye and just smile. It was a naughty but sweet smile.

One night a few of Terry's men came into the club. I could tell that something wasn't right and within a few minutes Terry was up and ready to leave. He kissed me on the cheek, said he had business to attend to and asked if I was okay to take a taxi home. I readily agreed and beckoned Sian over so I could order another drink. She leant right in so that I could whisper the order into her ear. I felt myself swoon under the sweet smell of her fragrance. I had never wanted anyone, ever, like I wanted her in that very minute. After I whispered what I wanted to drink I planted a kiss on her neck, just under her ear. She shuddered, giggled and then the intensity in her eyes told me that she felt the same. I stayed in the club until her shift finished. She asked me if I would like to come back to her flat for a coffee. I was up and ready to leave before she finished the sentence. The sexual tension between us raged all the way back to her home. In the taxi I just wanted to kiss her, but I knew Terry had eyes and ears everywhere and I would never have put Sian at risk. Once we stepped inside her front door, we were all over each other, kissing passionately and tugging furiously at each other's clothes. We were still licking, sucking and fucking well into the early hours. I didn't want to leave, but I knew that I had to. I was smitten with this beautiful Welsh girl, and I wanted more. Terry and I went to the club again a few weeks later, at my suggestion, and Sian was completely indifferent towards me. At first I thought it was an act in front of Terry, but I soon learnt that it wasn't. I managed to speak to her alone and asked if everything was alright. She smiled and said that she enjoyed the evening and that was it. It was a one-night stand. I was shattered. I could have expected that kind of indifferent behaviour from a man because, let's be fair, they've really mastered the art of impersonal sex. I have known scores of women from the clubs fall for some sweet talker only to discover that once the deed has been done, that was it. I felt awkward, confused and filled with a kind of emptiness but, I was determined to retain my grace and dignity and so I taught myself not to feel bad about the whole experience but embrace it for what it was and just giggle quietly to myself at how naughty I had been," Shirley said as she swallowed the last of the red wine.

"I could just tear your clothes off!" thought Star. *"Get a grip!"*

There was a moment's awkward silence.

"I bought this for you," Shirley said eventually.

She reached down and handed star a one-pound bag of the black ivory coffee from Northern Thailand.

"I thought that you might enjoy this," said Shirley.

"Thank you, but you really shouldn't have," Star said before breathing in the fumes from the coffee beans.

"It's just coffee, Star, nothing else," said Shirley.

"Should I offer her another glass of wine?" thought Star. *"This could end up getting serious. I can't believe how I'm falling for Shirley. I have to stop and think this through."*

There was a second moment of awkward silence.

Shirley looked down at her watch.

"I have an appointment but thank you for your company and listening without judgement. Maybe, if it's okay with you, we can meet for a coffee or a glass of wine again, another time," Shirley said as she stood up and began walking towards the lounge doorway.

"Yes, of course, that would nice," said Star.

Her mouth was dry, and her heart was thumping against her chest. She hadn't felt that way since she had slept with Julia.

Star saw her to the front door.

"Will she try to kiss me? Should I kiss her on the cheek... what should I do?" thought Star.

Shirley stepped into the hallway, smiled and blew Star a kiss before turning on her heels and walking to the elevator. She couldn't help but notice how Shirley's dress hem was narrower than her waist which forced her to walk with a wiggle.

Chapter 22

Star had been driving through Kensington when she decided to stop and check to see if Tracey, the cleaner, was in Maude's apartment on her usual working day.

Star knocked on the door. She could hear movement inside the apartment. The door opened.

"Oh, it's you," hissed Tracey. "What do you want?"

"We need to talk about the money that's been taken from Maude's bank account, Tracey," Star said assertively.

With a look of horror Tracey tried to slam the door but Star quickly put her foot in the door. Tracey pushed and leant against the door, but it wouldn't close.

"You need to let me in," Star said as she pushed back against the door.

Finally, Tracey let go of the door and raced down the hallway. As Star entered the apartment a ceramic ornament flew past her head and smashed into small pieces against the wall behind her. Tracey threw a second object which Star just managed to avoid.

"I am a police officer, Tracey. I'm asking you nicely to stop throwing things and talk to me."

"You're all the bloody same!" Tracey yelled from the kitchen.

Star could hear the jumble of cutlery and dinnerware, so she stopped and peered around the kitchen door from the hallway.

Tracey stood by the sink with a large chef's knife that was generally used to slice and joint large cuts of beef. The eight-inch stainless steel blade glistened in the sunlight.

"Put the weapon down," Star said as she cautiously entered the kitchen with both hands held up. "There is no need for this. It can only end badly."

"You, Star bloody Bellamy, walk in here with your big smiles and designer dresses, going off to fancy restaurants and monthly jaunts to Claridges with her ladyship. I hate you and I despise people like you!"

"I'm sure we can talk this through, Tracey. Just put the weapon down." Star said calmly.

"You know nothing about me or what I've had to put up with. Rich bitches like you and Maude born with a silver spoon in your mouth, just swanning through life without a care in the world," Tracey said bitterly.

"Come on Tracey, put the weapon down," Star said as she took a single step forward.

"I've had to work hard all my life! Day in and day out I run around after the likes of Maude while they look down their noses at me. Tracey the cleaner, that's what they think. I'm Tracey, the bloody cleaner, who is not good for anything but cleaning up after them. Well, I've had enough and now it's my turn. It's time that I was rewarded for all the shit I've had to take."

"Just put the knife down Tracey and we can talk about this," Star said firmly.

"I deserve a better life," Tracey said as she nodded her head. "I deserve to have money in the bank, to not worry about paying bills. I deserve to have my own home, a fancy place like this in a nice part of town. I want to spend Christmas in New York, like Maude, or have the choice to spend my summers in Monaco and lounge around being waited on hand and foot. You have no idea what it's like to be in my shoes, to live my life. I have worked almost every day since I left school and now it's my turn to be living the high life."

"You've stolen Maude's money, Tracey. She has been good to you and gave you a job when you needed it most and she paid you more than the going rate. In your heart you know what you're doing isn't right. Just put the weapon down and we can try and work all this out," Star said as she took another small step closer to Tracey.

"A few hundred thousand pounds is nothing to Maude. I've seen all her bank accounts. It's obscene just how much money she has when people like me struggle to pay our bills and put food on the table. No, that is my money now. I'm entitled to it and there's nothing you can do about it!" Tracey said as she tightened her grip on the chef's knife.

"I'm not going to ask you again, Tracey. I'm a police officer, now put down your weapon and let's talk like civilised adults about this problem," Star said as she edged forward.

"Fuck you and fuck all that you stand for," yelled Tracey, and she ran forward slashing the knife from left to right.

Instinctively Star called upon all her Jiu Jitsu training. She blocked Tracey's frenzied slicing movement with a powerful left upper block and a firm right jab that landed with such ferocity that Tracey was thrown back against the kitchen cabinet.

"It's still not too late to just put the weapon down," Star said, as she lowered her defensive stance. "Come on Tracey, you really don't want to do this."

Tracey had been stunned, her eyes were red and filled with decades of bitterness, resentment and rage. With the chef's knife still firmly in her right hand she used her left hand to touch her mouth. When she looked down and saw blood, her eyes opened wider as she screamed out 'argh!" and ran forward, waving the huge blade back and forth. The knife narrowly missed Star's arm as she side-stepped Tracey's frantic stabbing movement. Star kicked her shin; Tracey buckled and lowered the knife. Star took a short step back before raising her right knee straight forward while keeping her foot hanging freely. With all the strength she could muster she straightened her leg and struck Tracey in the middle of her body. Star immediately retracted her leg as Tracey was sent sprawling across the ceramic tiled floor. Seeing that Tracey had dropped the knife and was gasping for air, Star raced across the kitchen. Still shaken, Tracey scrambled onto her knees and began crawling across the tiled floor, trying to get at the knife. Star threw herself on top of Tracey. Both her legs and arms collapsed with a thud as Star forced her weight down onto Tracey's back. Star grappled to bring Tracey's right arm behind her back.

"You're dead, bitch!" Tracey yelled as she fought back ferociously.

Star managed to slowly edge up Tracey's back and place her knee on the back of her neck. She paused before taking a deep breath and then yanked on Tracey's arm until it was hauled up and almost touch her neck.

"Arghhhh, that fucking hurts!" Tracey screamed out. "You posh bastards will never know what it's like to live my life!"

"Tracey North, I'm placing you under arrest on suspicion of theft. You do not have to say anything, but it may harm your defence if you do not mention, when questioned, something which you later rely on in court," Star said as she reached into her pocket for her mobile telephone.

DC Robin Carpenter answered, "Yes Sergeant?"

"I've just made an arrest for theft and the attempted murder of a police officer," Star said. "Can you get some uniforms here, please?"

Star gave Robin Maude's address

"We're on our way Sergeant!"

"This could have gone a lot easier, Tracey," Star said as she placed her handcuffs on Tracey.

"Easier? You mean that I just carried on scrubbing posh people's homes for the rest of my days? It was my time to shine, my time to enjoy this good life that people like you and Maude just take for granted," Tracey said through gritted teeth.

"We all make choices Tracey. You had the choice to work hard at school, get qualifications and move on to university so you would get the skills that employers were prepared to pay for," said Star.

"Choices, what bloody choices did I have? I was born on a council estate in Southeast London. My mother, God rest her soul, had four children from four different men and none of them stuck around once she fell pregnant. My oldest sister, Clara, was raped and murdered when she was just fifteen and do you know what? It didn't even make the newspapers! Just another kid off the council estate, but if that happened here in Kensington then I'm sure the press, police and everyone else would have been up in arms," said Tracey.

Star remained quiet.

"What chance did I have of university? I had to leave school at fourteen to work so that food could be put on the table for the family to eat. My mother would disappear with her latest lover for days at a time leaving me to hold the creditors at bay, make sure that my youngest sisters got to school in a clean uniform. Choices. You make me laugh. I had no choices. Circumstance was thrust upon me, and I had to step up," Tracey said as a single tear streamed down her cheek.

"What happened to your mother?"

"She went out one day and just never came back. For all I know she could have been murdered and dumped in the Thames. Yeah, at just seventeen I had two siblings that were dependent on me."

"How are your sisters?"

"One is dead from a drug overdose brought on by her low life drug dealing pimp of a boyfriend and my youngest sister, Rhonda, packed up her bags and left for Spain and I haven't heard from or seen anything of her since the day she walked out. So no, Star Bellamy, I didn't have any of those choices that people like you love to spout on about," said Tracey.

"Have you ever spoken to anyone?"

"Like who? Who would truly have given a shit if I had marched off down to social services when my mother fucked off? My sisters would have been taken into care and I would have been out on my ear so the family home would go to someone else. The only choice I had was to work hard at anything that came my way but it's not enough. Have you any idea how hard it is to open a fridge with just milk and a few bits of scraps in it when the people I work for throw away more out of date food in a week than I put in my shopping basket? Maude has a bottle of brandy in that cabinet over there that costs more than my month's salary. I would have to work a whole day for that little drop that she treats herself to every night. It's sickening and wrong on all levels," said Tracey.

"The system isn't perfect, Tracey, but that doesn't give you the right to steal Maude's money," Star said as she shook her head.

"Why not! Why the fuck not? The tax man takes the working person's taxes at source, while rich people employ smart, underhanded accountants to avoid tax. Isn't that theft but on a grander scale?"

Star found herself nodding.

"Yet nobody with any power blinks at eye at them. The rich stay rich and the poor just work and die. None of them are trustworthy, they're all in it for what they can get and that's the politicians, banks and big business. Then they go and employ people like you to arrest relatively minor criminals and plaster it all over the newspapers that yet another deprived kid off the council estate gets sent to prison while Mr X who has just set up an offshore business sends all his profits overseas and pays zero tax. In my view they're the real crooks, the real criminals and those that harm society most."

"You make an interesting and debatable, point, Tracey, but none of it justifies you stealing money from Maude," Star said as she helped Tracey off the carpet and sat her on the sofa.

***

Star looked out of the window and saw that a police car had arrived along with DC Robin Carpenter.

"So, that's it now for me," Tracey said as she lowered her head. "I'll be bundled off to prison alongside all the other working-class stiffs who just wanted a taste of what you, the rich, take for granted."

Star left the kitchen and jogged down the hallway to open the front door.

"Are you okay, Sergeant?" DC Robin Carpenter said as he looked Star up and down.

"Yes, I'm fine thank you. She's in the kitchen," Star said as she turned to the uniformed officers.

Tracey was led down the hallway by the two police officers. She stopped and looked directly in Star's eyes.

"The day will come when the working-class poor from across the world will rise up and fight back against this bankrupt capitalist system that serves only to keep the poor in poverty and protect the morally corrupt rich," Tracey snarled.

"That revolution may or may come not come. I said that you had choices, we all do. Your biggest mistake, Tracey, was your lack of belief in your own abilities to become more than the hand you got dealt. I can give you a real-life example. The author, JK Rowling was a divorced single mother of three and relied on the benefit system to make ends meet. That incredibly talented woman battled through abuse, depression and I believe she even contemplated suicide. Despite all the challenges that life had thrown at her she refused to accept failure and made time, even with three young children, for her writing. She had a choice, just as you did, but you, Tracey, chose to steal from the woman who showed you kindness and paid your wages," Star said before motioning the officer to take Tracey away.

DC Robin Carpenter followed Star through to the lounge where she spotted Tracey's black handbag. She reached in and found a plastic bottle of Diazepam tablets.

"This explains Maude's sudden health issues," thought Star.

Star reached into Maude's bag again and pulled out a brown envelope. It hadn't been sealed, so she took out the document and began to read it. Star's eyes widened as it dawned on her that Tracey was in possession of a fake last will and testament that named her the sole beneficiary to Maude's fortune. It just needed Maude's signature.

"She was planning to murder, Maude" thought Star.

***

Star followed the police car back to the station where she telephoned Miles, Maude's nephew, and told him that Tracey North had been arrested. She asked for him to call in at the police station and ask for Detective Constable Robin Carpenter so he could take a statement.

Star began to filter through the mountain of paperwork on her desk when she heard the sound of footsteps racing across the open plan office and towards her door.

Knock... Knock!

"Yes, come in," Star said as she placed her pen on the desk.

"Sergeant, its Camden White," said DC Sally York.

"What about him?" Star said as she straightened her back and sat upright.

"We've just heard that he was found hanging in his cell this morning," said DC Sally York.

"Murdered?"

"No, Sergeant. The guards opened his cell door this morning and found him hanging. He's dead," said DC Sally York.

"Is there anything to suggest that this is not a suicide?" said Star.

"They are treating it as a suicide but..."

"But what?" Star said as she motioned Sally to finish her sentence.

"It seems strange and maybe more than a coincidence that all three of the security cameras along the cell block were found to have malfunctioned," said Sally.

"What about the footage?"

"I asked the same question Sergeant, and the answer that came back was that the footage was unusable," said Sally.

"Three cameras?" Star said with a quizzical look.

"Yes Sergeant. I was informed that they were sent off to the crime laboratory for analysis," said Sally.

"This all sounds incredibly convenient," Star said.

"It sounds as if everyone is dead set on this being a suicide, Sergeant," said Sally.

"You bloody played me, Shirley Fenton, this was justice, Fenton style," thought Star.

***

Sally left the office and Star leant back into her chair. Her mobile phone rang. It was an unknown caller, but instinct compelled her to answer the call.

"This is Detective Sergeant Star Bellamy, who is this?"

"How nice to hear your voice again, Star, it has been a long time, too long," a woman's voice said. "My name is Daphne. Daphne Edwards and I was a great friend of your mother's. I remember you as just a little girl."

"I'm sorry but your name is only vaguely familiar. You say that you and my mother were friends?" Star said.

Daphne replied, "We were and still are but that's a story for another time. We have to meet, Star."

"I need to know how you knew my mother," Star said

"Your mother and I are both members of the Grand Order of Pythia." Daphne said.

"The Grand order of Pythia?"

"Surely your mother told you about the Grand Order of Pythia," Daphne said.

"She did once, and when I asked her about it she would always say 'all in good time'," Star said.

Daphne said, "Star, I witnessed your psychic abilities when you were just a child. Your mother, my friend, was the most powerful of the Pythia. She must have told you that one day you will be called upon?"

"She did say something like that. It all seems kind of vague now."

"You witnessed an apparition recently, Star, and there will be more, only far more powerful. The Grand Order of the Pythia needs you. Danger is coming..." Daphne said.

Chapter 23

Detective Inspector Ronald Pratt took a taxicab from his mother's home in Shoreditch into the city where he had been invited to meet Chief Superintendent Raymond Nichols and fellow senior brethren at The Trinity, a private members club. Ronald wore a black pin stripe suit that he had tailor made in Saville Row especially for functions outside of the lodge. He felt smart and important in his crisp handmade shirt and highly polished black brogues. The City of London private member's clubs are the epitome of luxury and an institution that Ronald recognised as the most exclusive and elusive organisations in the world. The Trinity club was the most exclusive of all, with family memberships dating back almost a century.

The taxicab stopped outside the club. Ronald could feel his heart thumping as he stared up in awe at the club's grand entrance. A doorman dressed in a royal blue suit with gold braid around the neck and gold buttons down the front opened the taxi door and smiled.

"Good evening, Mr Pratt. We were told to expect you."

"Good evening," DI Pratt said stiffly. "I believe my friend Raymond Nichols is expecting me."

"He is sir. If you'd like to follow me," the doorman said as he motioned Ronald to follow him.

Ronald tried to keep his eyes on the doorman as he passed from one opulent room into another. A tall man in his late forties approached him. He wore a tailor made, charcoal grey, three-piece suit. Ronald noticed that despite his early years he had combed his thinning grey hair over his receding hair line.

"Good evening, Mr Pratt. My name is Charles Gobain, and I am the Executive Director of our private member's club. Welcome."

Ronald shook his hand firmly.

"I'll show you through to Mr Nichols' private suite," Charles Gobain said as he turned swiftly on his heels and led Ronald through a pair of panelled doors into a large dark oak panelled room with an open fireplace. In the middle of the room was a large boardroom style table with nine antique Carver chairs. There were eight smartly dressed men standing around the fireplace holding brandy glasses.

"Ah, Ronald. How lovely that you could join us, thank you," Raymond Nichols said with a broad smile. "Let me introduce you to some friends. This is Hugo, Harvey, Thomas, Edward, Theo and Franklin. Gentlemen this is Worshipful Master Ronald Pratt."

"Good evening, nice to meet you, worshipful master," said Hugo.

"Please, it's Ronald," Ronald said as he shook each of their hands.

"Charles," Raymond Nichols called.

"Sir?"

"Could we have a bottle of Louis XIII Black Pearl and a Lecompte Secret Calvados and then a little privacy?" Raymond Nichols said as he motioned his guests to take a seat at the table. "Do you like a Calvados, Ronald?"

"I'm not sure that I've ever had one, Raymond," Ronald said awkwardly.

"Well, we all have mixed views here. Thomas, Franklin and I enjoy a good cognac while the others prefer the Calvados. Just like the traditional brandies, the Calvados production is limited to a specific region only, it is distilled in Normandy from apples. Personally, I find it tastes like a hard cider and it simply doesn't suit my palate," Raymond said with a tone of authority.

"You're just a brandy snob," snapped Thomas.

"Yes I am, and proud to be one my friend. Ronald," Raymond said, as he caught Charles Gobain's eye, "Let Charles pour you a glass of the Black Pearl."

"Thank you, Raymond," Ronald said as he sat at the table.

Charles placed the glass of brandy on the table by Ronald.

"Gentleman, can I be of any further service?" said Charles.

Raymond glanced quickly around the table and smiled.

"No, that will be all, Charles."

Raymond waited until the twin oak panelled doors were closed firmly.

"Before we start, Ronald, I wanted to personally congratulate you for solving the Fenton case. That was a nasty business, but it was extremely well managed throughout. Well done," said Raymond.

"Hear, hear," Thomas and Hugo said.

"With your help and guidance, Ronald, that assertive young Detective Sergeant, Star Bellamy, appears to have performed well. The Fenton family described her as having an abundance of charm, but beneath her warm, welcoming, smile, lurked a powerful, driven, police officer. They were grateful for your help. I understand that the murderer has since taken his own life and so closes another episode. Your hard work, diligence and commitment to both the police force and the masonic order has not gone unnoticed. You are just weeks away from your Chief Inspector's role and, Ronald, we have ambitions for you well beyond that," Raymond said as he smiled and slowly nodded his head.

"Thank you, Raymond," Ronald said as he looked around the table. "Thank you, brothers."

"I spoke to you in confidence after your installation as worshipful master, Ronald, and I told you then that plans were being drawn up and there would come a time when you may be called upon. Do you recall that?"

"I do, Raymond, and I confirmed then that I was ready to serve you and the craft,"

"Good, because brother, that time has come," Raymond muttered darkly. "We are in the midst of a war with the hard line left."

"Have you seen the television programmes and adverts, Ronald?" said Hugo.

Ronald shook his head.

"Almost overnight, the adverts are pandering to the left with zero or only a few white actors. The family scenes are portrayed as mixed race and most recently there have been others that deliberately set out to emasculate men," Hugo said, staring pointedly at Ronald.

"They are attacking the very foundations of British society with their ideology. The two-parent family unit where a woman actually wants to marry a man and have children, with established, traditional roles is now deemed alien," said Thomas.

"The far left despise the very notion of little boys and girls. Their war is with biology, human nature and reality," said Franklin.

Ronald nodded.

"The youngsters are like sheep and aimlessly fall for this fad of believing that being fluid is cool," said Thomas.

"There is talk, behind closed doors in parliament," Theo said curtly, "of no longer being able to say he and she."

"Utterly ridiculous," said Hugo.

"It is, but the extreme left are amassing political muscle to alter reality by force," Theo said as he reached for his brandy glass.

"That is just the tip of the iceberg, Ronald," said Raymond." There are strategic moves with far-left rioters setting fires in cities, vandalising buildings, attacking police officers and leaving some of them hospitalised for simply doing their duty. These actions are being co-ordinated and organised by idealistic radicals with powerful political and financial muscle. They are calling on their influential friends in the media to taint the facts and hide the criminal violence perpetrated by violent mobs by making it look as if it's the police who are at fault to further support their aims and objectives."

There was a moment's silence around the table as Raymond's words sank in.

"They are trying to re-write history, gentlemen. Whilst none of us condone some of the actions carried out by people who have long since passed, it did happen. It is wrong to wipe it away but rather to learn from the mistakes," said Harvey.

"It's deplorable what's happening," said Hugo.

"The Marxist anarchists genuinely believe that they are patriots ushering in a new age," Raymond said as he scanned the room and watched the brethren unanimously nod in agreement.

"What can we do?" Ronald said innocently.

"We are many, Ronald, and just as the soviets tried to beat, bully and stamp out the belief in God with forced atheism, the soviet ideology lost. In this idealistic battle we will be providing a helping hand by utilising our own key people in prominent, powerful, positions."

"How can I help?" Ronald said with a crooked grin.

"My brothers and I," said Raymond. "Have identified the top one hundred most powerful and influential people co-ordinating and supporting the left agenda and like a surgeon's blade, as he cuts out a cancer, our actions will be decisive, highly focused and targeted."

Books by Jayne Gooding

The Thick Blue Line

The Thick Blue Line II

The Thick Blue Line III

The Climb

Horns & Halos

Horns & Halos: Born Bad (Coming Soon!)

Facebook: Jayne Gooding Author

Website: www.jaynegooding.com

Printed in Great Britain
by Amazon